a little tiff between love and money...

Pyaar se peyt nahi bharta!!

Marshall the IIIrd presents

a little tiff between love and money...

Pyaar se peyt nahi bharta!!

Nishtha Chatterjee

Publisher
UNICORN BOOKS
F-2/16, Ansari Road, Daryaganj, New Delhi-110002
☎ 011-23275434, 23262683, 23250704 • *Fax:* 011-23257790
E-mail: info@unicornbooks.in • *Website:* www.unicornbooks.in

Branch : Mumbai
23-25, Zaoba Wadi, Thakurdwar, Mumbai-400002
☎ 022-22010941, 022-22053387
E-mail: rapidex@bom5.vsnl.net.in

ISBN 978-81-7806-375-1

Edition: 2015

Printed at : Param Offsetters, Okhla, New Delhi-110020

Pyaar se peyt nahi bharta!!

This is my first written endeavour as a fiction writer, & it comes from my heart as well as my experiences in the colourful city of Delhi.

I would like to request you all to please be kind enough to ignore writing flaws, if any, as this is my maiden venture and a lot of disturbing influences were involved in the making of this book.

Also, this book is meant not for a niche audience, but regular everyday types like you & me, who are into sms & whatsapp slangs and proud usage of Hinglish. So if you are the prudish type, and expect Shakespearean style of prose and poetry, please steer clear of this book right away, lest you regret later!

I hope you enjoy reading 'Pyaar se peyt nahi bharta' and are kind enough to recommend my efforts to your friends and family.

Enjoy reading!!

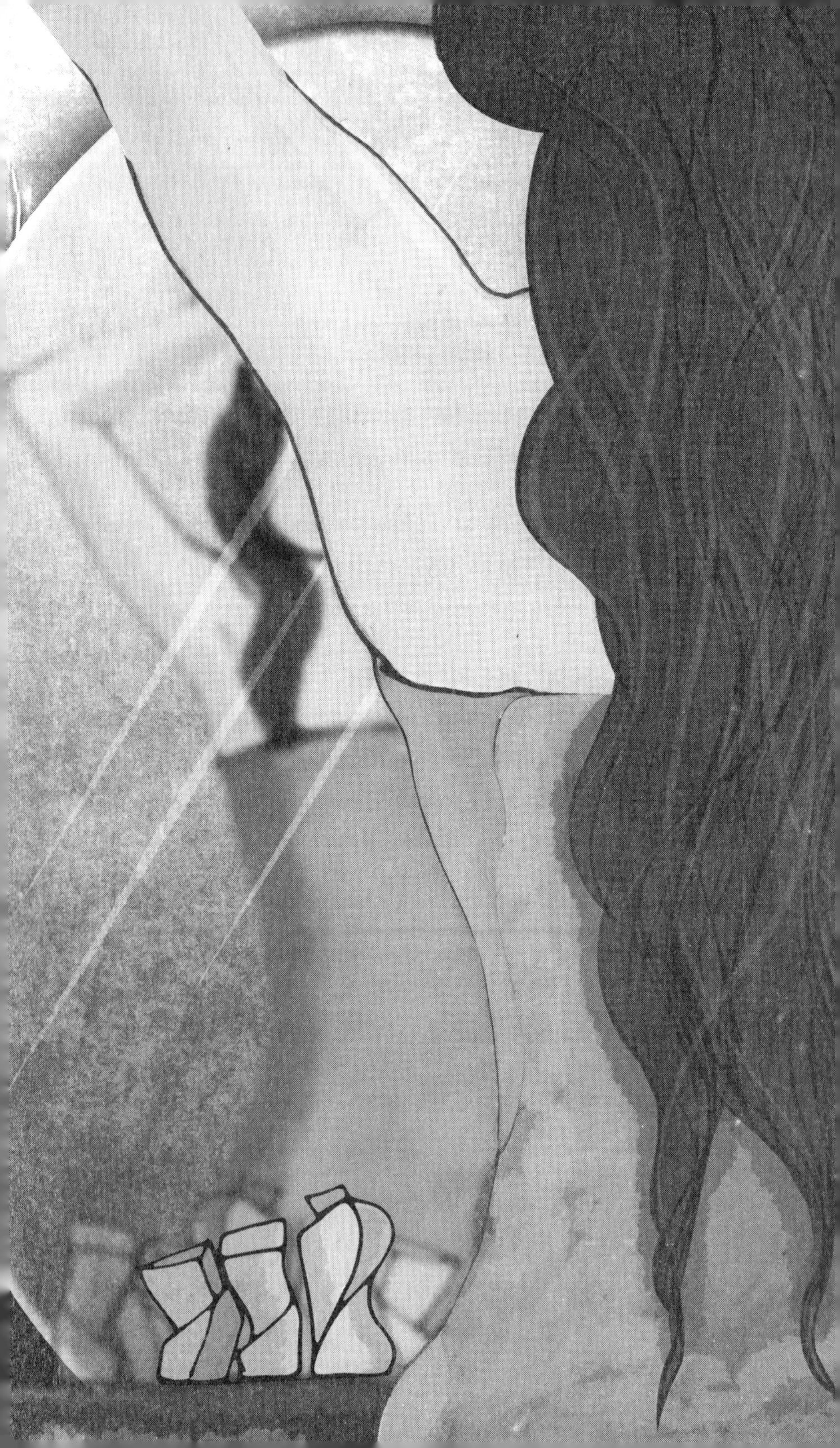

THE INCIDENT

Body lotion, fairness cream, hair lotion, perfume, nail paint, another nail paint for toe nails, lip gloss, mascara, eye liner, rings, ear rings, watch, bracelet…,after using 23 beauty products and 18 number of accessories, she was ready, ready for just another regular day of her life.. "Sneh.. Sneh Sharma". Usually her days would start with two glasses of lukewarm water, some toilet reading (anything except the newspaper) and attending college, taking lectures, making notes, little hangouts before and after classes, coffee, snacking, internet, SMSes, facebook and power naps at home that would turn into hours.

But not every day is usual!

Around 2:30, after 1 hour and 20 minutes of continuously listening to her teacher about how one anthropologist negates the concepts of another, whereas a third one gives an altogether new critique to the theory, all this while expecting the students to later go to the library and search like crazy for each of their books and make exhaustive notes for it, her glass was full, spilling already. Her thoughts started to drip in all directions, most of them filled with questioning the teacher..

"Why would she become a teacher at such young age?.. Isn't a person supposed to do something with whatever one has learned and starts teaching others only after getting old? Or after achieving a lot? Look at her nails and make up..maybe she wanted to become a model, but her parents wouldn't let her start from the bra panties catalogue at mayantra.com. Maybe she is a part time model, maybe she's here just to lure us girls into some sex racket and being a teacher is just her fake identity.. yes!"

Before her imagination could go further weird, she decides to quit, She gives out an eye gesture to her friend that meant "let's just get the hell out of here!" and took the cap off from the back of her pen, put it on the front, flip closed her notebook, zipped up her bag to zip out of the classroom and have some fresh air that does not contain any knowledge particles for a while.

Her quitting in the middle of the class did not go well with the model material multifaceted teacher, knowing exactly what's happening, she complainingly asked Sneh.. "WHAT IS YOUR NAME?"

"Sneh Sharma" she replied as she walked towards the door, thinking she needs to spend some time with people who at least know her name. Her friend too got up from her desk and said

"My name is Thoibi"..

Teacher: Who asked your name?

"Oh.. I just thought, i'll tell you as I'm leaving as well" she said following Sneh.

Unfortunately, the outside of the class was almost as boring as the inside, plus the blistering heat! Everyone was doing their own thing, mostly chatting in a group of less than 8, divided into half rich-ass cool and half lower middle class not so cool students looking up and looking down at each other.

From the outside any college would look like a beautiful family of students having the best times of their lives, but inside..it's a nation, with different states, divides, egos, politics, racism and crisis.. nah, it's actually not "that" bad.

The only things that seemed to uplift Sneh and her friend's spirits were junk food and some potential shopping at Kamla Nagar market. So they took turns to use the rear view mirror of her car for their timely aesthetic adjustments, swinging to Bollywood music and "buy a flat in Noida" commercials on FM radio, they made their way to the market.

Kamla Nagar.. It's amazing how these roadside markets have a lot new to offer every single day, Sneh thought. Endless colours, food, rickshaws, stray dogs, students, aunties, hip aunties, vendors, cars with loud music with swagger guys in them, hand in hand couples, little babies smiling at strangers walking behind their parents, all frying in the pan of Delhi heat.

After hustling through the crowd, outfits and accessories for more than 2 hours, girls stopped at a "*gol gappe wala bhaiya*" who was already busy satisfying more ladies than an average Indian male would in his lifetime.

Just as she looked at her watch, it hit Sneh's friend that she is getting late for something. Well, not a deal breaker for Sneh's golgappa binge, she asked *bhaiya* to give her one plate only, and asked her friend to have at least some, so she just popped one in her mouth quickly and left saying "boOye" with her mouth full.

While Sneh was in her partial trance having *gol gappe*, she realized a guy among other guys from the other side of the road, next to a BMW is throwing awkward smiles at her. He kept looking at her again and again while having his overly expressive conversation enriched with evil laughs and high fives. Sneh tried to remember if she knows him from somewhere as he looked familiar.

It was annoying, but no big deal, happens all the time in Delhi, BUT! as soon as she tried to look away from him rotating her face swirling her tongue in the awesome combo of spicy liquid and crunch..

Dhoinngg!!

There is this other guy, staring at her, much closer than the other one, from about 10 feet away from her. While the previous guy was standing possessively close to a BMW and was in almost colour blocking branded apparel, this other guy was one cheap-ass lowly, road side type guy in V-shaped old "*ghisi-hui*" *chappals* and office pants that probably had roamed through many generations before having their pursuit on him and his shirt had some embroidered school patch on the pocket but it was somehow clear that he never went to any. He was around 19, 20 maybe but was so weak, having wrists of an anorexic and was short, making it hard to guess his age.

His stare was different, it was shameless, as if he is not doing anything wrong but great, not the regular stare you get in Delhi, too creepy to let go off and carry on..bit too intense, like she owes him the pleasures he's having looking at her body. Still it's not perverted enough to stop her from eating, but she does simultaneously planned to teach him a lesson as soon as she finishes.

He continued starting at her, down to up that further lead to her anger.

So here it was, final *gol gappa* swallowed, mouth and hands wiped, 50 rupees given, return amount taken!

About 8 fast charging steps towards him..

She: *KYA DEKHRA HAI BE? SLAP! HEIN??? SLAP!*

Him: *Kuch nahi* (curling his body like an embryo to avoid more slaps)

She: *KUCH NAHI?.. GHUUUR KISKO RAHA HAI?..*

She grabs a handful of his forehead hair puff to get him straight again..

Him: *Nahi main to dekhra tha bus..*

She: *KYAAA DEKH RAHA THAA? Kab se dekh rahi hun ghuure ja raha hai UPAR SE NICHE, NICHE SE UPAR.*

Him: *Main tou bus road pe dekhra…*

She: *ACHA?*

Few other guys came closer to take over the situation and probably beat the shit out of him..but she made a gesture showing that everything is under her control and she did not need any help, but still crowd started to build up as if it was some Bollywood shooting.

She was now holding his wrist so he won't run away, just as he got his breath back from the two slaps, he continued..

"Woh bhi tou dekh raha tha.." pointing at the other guy.. (who was not there anymore, but she knows who he is talking about)

She: *Beta woh college ke bahar khada tha..nahaya hua tha.. kuch kaam karta hoga.. ya student hoga.. shayed mere hee college ka ho..shayed mujhe jaanta hee ho.. "*

He (interrupting her): *Kaam tou main bhi karta hun!..nahaya bhi tha.. kal.. main Jai Ambe Properties pe kaam karta hun.. makaan dikhane ka..*

"Golgappe khate hue hee tou dekh raha tha!..Bees rupaye tou main bhi de sakta hun.. matlub chalis.. bees mere bhi!"

This proud statement from him shook her and took her by such a surprise that she was out of words or actions for about 7 seconds. She felt embarrassed, humiliated with the fact that he actually believes that he is good enough for her, and to his practical assessment, she felt like giving him a practical disagreement.

She then shoots her reply which she had thought of in those 7 shocked seconds

"*Main yahan sirf gol gappe khane nahi ayi thi, wo tou bus mera mann kargeya tha, main Berkos ja rahi thi*, pointing towards its giant vertical billboard, *chal!..CHALEGA SATH?.. CHALEIN?..CHAL LE?* She started to tug him from his wrist towards the restaurant.

He twisted his wrist out of her hand with a jerk and gave her another shocker..*"Chalo!"*

Crowd started to disperse in disappointment, their dose of cheap thrills seemed to be over as Sneh and the accused made their way towards the restaurant and took its stairs.

Berkos (name changed :p) was no 5 star or anything, but this little Chinese restaurant and Bar was still way out of budget of that guy or of common masses.

THE FIRST DATE?

As soon as they entered Berkos, he felt as if he has landed on another planet, a planet which lacked oxygen, light and had lower gravity than the earth. He could hardly see far due to the dim lights, there was this shiny brittle crockery and fragrance of Chinese food mixed with people wearing branded perfumes all around. But to him it was just a matter of one question "Whether he will be able to pay the bill or not?"

He had some Rs.400 and some coins (I mention the coins as he had a good bunch that would sum up to around 80) and he had felt that it would be enough for any restaurant meal. The only restaurant he had visited earlier was MkDonalds, and that too just to use their washroom.

Both of them had little idea of what was happening, he for some reason calculated this moment into a game that if he could pay this bill, he would prove to his ego that he was good enough to at least look at her.

They sat on a small table for 2 people. He did not have the guts to ask for a menu, but she nonetheless placed one in front of him in a sarcastic way, and ordered very little, but while she did, he tried to read the tongue twisting names of dishes with the little English he could read. Alongside he calculated that if he takes the same of what she has ordered, it will be around Rs.380, which was close, but under his limits.

They didn't converse, rather she took out her swanky smart phone and updated her Facebook status to "You won't believe WTF is happening @ Berkos", to which she immediately started receiving likes and comments from people who have no life! They ate sans any conversation, but only some angry stares from Sneh and some pleading innocent look-aways from him. She was rather amazed at what exactly she was doing with this lowly guy, but still thought it would be fun once they will finish eating, and he will be humiliated due to his inability to pay the bill amount.

While this guy was still to figure what he is eating, she finished her plate. But those were only the starters! She asked for the menu again!

Dhoinngg!!!

To him it felt like sitting on a giant wheel cart coming down from its highest point with a furious swing. Now he started to sweat, all the air conditioners now ineffective for him. She noticed the look on his face and shot out another dose of sarcasm..*"Paise hain na tumhare paas?"*

He just managed to respond with a low *"hmm"*. This little *"hmm"* made her more cautious so she called back the waiter and ordered the most expensive dishes on the menu, to fool-proof her plan of teaching him a lesson, lest he has some amount of money on him and her plan backfires! She ordered 2 Briizers, knowing very well that the drinks will definitely skyrocket the bill amount.

After a long eating session with the mute on, she finally got verbal..*"Tum ghuur kyun rahe the? Kya milta hai tum logo ko ghuur ke? Tumhe kya lagta hai aise ladki khush hogi? Ya pat jaegi?"*

He: *"Nahi main ghuur nahi raha tha. Main bas wahan client ka wait kar raha tha, wahan bas traffic tha, kutte the, showroom tha, ek gol-gappe ki redi thi aur aap the tou main bus sab kuch dekh raha tha..jab tak ki client aa jaata.."*

She: *Matlub mujhe dekhke timepass kar raha tha? Main timepass hun tum logon ka?*

He lowered his eyes and both of them got back to the mute eating mode again.

She finished the last few gulps of her Briizer and got up to use the washroom. Maybe it was the under 5.0 alcohol and too much food or just with the passage of time, her anger had faded away a little, before leaving for the washroom, she said to him *"Mere washroom se wapis aane tak nikal le yahan se.. Maaf kar rahi hun aaj tujhe, warna police ke paas le jaati.."*

When she came back after 10 minutes, the guy was not there. She took a deep breath, and settled down to regain some calm while she checked notifications on Facebook. The whole episode flashed before her eyes where she was grabbing his hair and slapping him, she had never in her life done anything like that before. She was half proud too that she has this side of herself to handle people when she has to.

She raised her hand to call the waiter for the bill.

Waiter: Anything else ma'm?

She: No, just the check please..

Waiter: Your bill has been paid ma'am.

She: What!!

Waiter: Yes ma'am, your friend said he has to leave. So he made the payment and left a while back.

Sneh: Ohhh OK.

She stood up and walked out slowly thinking about what an awkward day she has had.

What she did not know was that the waiter had actually lied to her. What happened there was a "Man-to-Man favour", which is a kind of favour that every guy would do for another guy in a situation of crisis that involves a pretty girl. For instance, if a guy wants to buy a pack of condoms as he is planning to have a wild night at some club, but has lost his wallet, I'm pretty sure some other random guy would buy them for him happily, rather, the chemist would give it to him for free (with a wicked grin of course) .. 'Man to Man favour'.

So what had actually happened was that as soon Sneh left to use the washroom, he rushed to the waiter to talk to him about his situation. *"Yaar main na Jai Ambe Properties pe kaam karta hun, ye le card chahe phone karke puuch le. Ladki ke saath pehli baar aaya hun, bill ke puure paise nahi hain, par abhi tu itne rakh le main bas ek ghante baad baaki de jaunga pakka! Ladki se kehna bill de gaya hun*. The waiter was more shocked by this guy's luck at having struck a date with such a hot girl, rather than what he had requested for,but nonetheless managed to say *"Chal theek hai, par ek ghante mein de jaio."*

Sneh drove back with her stomach too full and her head a little heavy with the drinking and the weird day thinking that she would probably never see this guy again and even if she did she would totally ignore him, all this while wondering if this did end up like a date? She promised herself that she would never be this creative again in trying to teach any random person a lesson.

Meanwhile the poor guy's ordeal was not over yet, as he still had to pay Rs.3600 to Berkos within an hour.

So he went to his property dealer boss and told him that he is dating a high society girl, and needed some money. And guess what did the boss say? No, he did not say no! Neither did he ask him how he was planning to return this hefty sum. He just lent him the money plus some extra bucks appreciating him saying *"Waah beta, abhi tou aaye hue chhe mahine bhi nahi hue aur launde ne baazi maar lii!..SHbasHH!"*..Another 'Man to Man Favour'

COINCIDENCE

More than 2 months later, 9th November, perfectly placed on Saturday by God, as It's Sneh's birthday and she's at Kamla Nagar again, the same place where that awkward *"durghatna"* took place. She was treating her friends at Berkos, irrespective of all the resistance from them as they wanted to go somewhere else. But it is her birthday and this restaurant is her favourite. As they crossed the same *gol gappe wala*, her eyes darted in all directions looking for the weird guy she met on that fateful day. More of looking for not to find him and preparing an appropriate reaction just in case she sees him again.

Cake, candles, food, drinks, smiles, laughter, silly jokes, pictures, some more drinks, pictures in even sillier poses, instagrams, uploads, just another regular birthday treat mixed with some inquisitive looks from a guy standing far, who looked like a ghost, straight from a Japanese horror movie, the waiter from that day. Who still couldn't stop wondering what was this girl doing with that guy that day. Fortunately for her, she did not encounter that strange guy anywhere near the restaurant or in the market.

After having fun and laughter till late afternoon, she was back home, exhausted answering numerous birthday wish calls and planning another party in the evening for another set of friends. She decided to take a power nap, which actually turned out to be a 2 hour long siesta, but this time, got disturbed by the ringing door bell. She gathered herself and somehow got up to see from the balcony who is downstairs, that's when she got the rudest birthday surprise..

Dhoingggg!!

What the..

It was the same weird guy from that day! Standing at her door! She was rather surprised at his courage to come directly to her house like that, filled with anger she stomped down the staircase and opened the door with a big swift pull. The guy immediately stepped back, and before he could have regained his composure or even recognize her, she barged at him, *"TERI ITNI HIMMAT KI TU SIIDHA MERE GHAR TAK AA GAYA?"*

It didn't take much time for him to be reminded of who she was..

He (still taking backward steps in defense): *Main tou... main tou address puuch raha tha. Mujhe nahi pata ki aap yahan rehte ho. Maine client ko ghar dikhaana tha, mujhe nahi pata ye aapka ghar hai.*

Now she did remember him telling her something about his job as an assistant to some property dealer, though she was a little apprehensive now that he does know where she lives. She feared that he could stalk her.

She: *Konsa address? Dikha* (Took the slip from his hand). *Nahi ye hamara nahi hai..ye aage next lane mein padrega.*

He then just said thank you and started moving towards his destination when he was stopped by a voice from behind *"OYE SUNN!"*

He turned around to find her still standing there.

"Iss area mein aur koi ghar khali hai kya rent ke liye?" Meri ek friend ko chahiye.

He: *Haan bohot hain.*

She: *Wo shaam ko mere ghar ayegi 5 baje. Tou dikha dio jara.. Aur ghuurio mat usko!*

He: *Haan theek hai* (he said hiding his scornful smile and left).

BIRTHDAY EVE

He reached her house before time and waited patiently outside. He was so used to of waiting for long durations for clients at various places. In fact he had started liking this activity, he would just stand for hours looking at random people, kind of studying the lifestyle of Delhiites. What they wear, how they move , what they eat et al. Inside he wanted to be like them someday, affluent, stylish, wealthy, and not being someone to be looked down upon.

As he was lost day-dreaming, a black safari stops with a screech and bass coming out of its stereo. As soon as the car doors opened, a strong whiff of expensive perfume floated out along with a dozen boys and girls who were spilling out of the car like cockroaches do when you spray their abodes with insecticide, except they were not struggling for their lives, rather seemed to be enjoying every bit of it. Some of them were holding gift boxes and bags. Sneh opened the gate of her house and there was an almost stampede like commotion with everyone trying to hug her, the girls shrieking birthday wishes in their shrilly voices, and the guys laughing heartily in their newly acquired heavy baritone adolescent voices. He was quietly standing a good 10 meters away, observing all this commotion with a mild smile on his face when she suddenly noticed him and said *"Bas thodi der mein aate hain."*

She came back in roughly around 20 minutes with her friend, and as soon as she opened the gate, she saw this guy was holding a gift pack in his hand, and meekly said "Happy Badday" in his rustic tone. She was so freaked out that she did not know how to react to this, so she shut her eyes tightly for 3 seconds and opened them just to say "Hmm thank you", before putting the gift carelessly on the stairs.

ohhhhh

Her friend: Oh nice! The dealer guy knows your birthday too!

Sneh (avoiding everything that could waste her party time): Let us just go and check this place out for you. Now since Sneh's friend was not well-versed with Hindi plus the ever prevailing fears of molestation, Sneh had to tag along when they visited 5 rooms at different floors in different lanes of the same area. After looking at some disappointing rooms to live in, he told them that this is the last option, and it's on the fourth floor. Already tired of room hopping, Sneh somehow climbed up but was badly out of breath, just being able to utter "Oh..I..I.. cannot go inside. I need some water." The guy fetched her some water from the family living on the floor below, and showed the room to her friend while Sneh tried to catch her breath in the balcony.

Waiting for them outside, she recalled that day at Berkos when she had ordered food like a famished refugee just to take revenge on this guy, and how he actually paid for all that from his hard earned income. She felt kind of sorry for the poor guy and took out four thousand rupee notes to give him from her handbag and folded them in her hand. She saw that her friend has liked this last room and is already talking about the deal further. She then handed out the money to him. He was taken aback and told her to pay the token amount directly to the dealer, but she strongly told him *"Ye uss din ke hain. Chup chap lele nahi tou pitega"*. He took the money and promptly gave her 400 rupees change.

Before leaving, Sneh asked for his mobile number in case of a future requirement. It was only after typing his number on her phone she cared to ask his name..

"Suraj Kumar" he replies.

Later back home, after the party, although tired as hell, she was still left with some last joules of energy to open her gifts. For reasons unknown to her, she decided to open the gift pack from Suraj first, most of others were open branded bags anyway. She was rather curious to see what it has. Before ripping it open, she decided to guess the contents, by pressing, feeling, shaking, weighing it, & came to the strange conclusion that it does feel quite a bit like a pack of bread. She wondered if it could actually be a pack of bread, "how weird would that be" she thought. She opened it up and found a nice colourful kurta inside. It was beautiful, her favourite colour, nice print and everything, the only problem being that she already had the same one in her wardrobe! Firstly she was rather surprised and somewhat embarrassed for how this Suraj guy's choice could be exactly the same as hers, and secondly how could he afford a kurta worth 1400 rupees from his meagre salary. But, all these problems felt minor compared to what came next.

The kurta was not the only gift he had given her, as she flipped open the kurta to see it in full, guess what is green and rolled down on her bed?

A pack of Whisper Ultra Soft!

Her cheeks turn a bright shade of red with anger. She had always thought of herself to be one of those, very hard to piss people, but this guy Suraj was doing it consistently and effortlessly. She realized that instead of burning her insides, now she has his number and could call him.

She called him to hear a caller tune that goes something like *"Oooooooooo huzoor tera tera tera suroooooooor..."* which made her look at her phone in disgust but nonetheless be patient for him to answer. And as soon as he did, she almost shouted in the mouthpiece

"SALEY!, YE KYA DIYA HAI TUUNE MUJHE?

Suraj: *Kyun? kurta hai.. aur..*

Sneh: *AUR, AUR KYA?"*

Suraj: *Aur wo packet mein kuch, mujhe tou pata nahi"*

Sneh: *Pata nahi? FIR DIYA KYUN HAI?"*

Suraj: *Wo dukaan pe pada tha tou main ne bola dikhaane ko tou dukan wala kehta nahi ye ladkiyon ki cheez hai. Tou main ne kaha ladki ko hee tou dena hai. Akela kurta bohot chhota sa tha, tou gift bada karne ke liye.. kyun kuch kharab nikla kya?*

There she was flabbergasted again! Unable to come with a reaction, she just ceased the 'sanitary' topic and asked him why did he give her a kurta so expensive.

He blatantly replies *"Nahi wo tou 250 rupaye ka hai"*

Sneh: *"Kya? 250? Bakwaas mat kar! Mere paas same kurta hai jo me ne 'WW' se liya tha..1400 ka hai. Wapis le ja usko shayad wapis hojaye.. Warna apni kisi behen ko de diyo, mujhe nahi chahiye.*

Suraj: *Nahi, main ne tou road se lia tha 150 ka. 250 bola taaki aapko bura na lage. Aap rakh lo pehenna mat chahe. Jab duusra wala purana hojaye tab nikaal lena ye wala."*

Sneh could just let out a sigh *"Phew, chal kal main teri dukaan pe aungi room ki payment dene aur tujhe wapis kardungi. Bas. Bye."*

She rolled back the Whisper pack into the kurta and dropped back on the bed.

DREAM SEQUENCE

Deserted on a desert, She's riding a camel and Suraj is her camel guy walking beside with heavy steps holding the steering rope. They are lost!

Out of food, water and breath and the sun flares which look awesome on music videos are now blinding their eyes. After a few dizzy steps, the camel comes to a halt, helpless, it drops to its knees and asks them for a Redbul or he won't move any further. Watching the camel quit like that, she falls flat on her face as well and gives up all hope to survive this rather strange ordeal. She cries out in a husky voice demanding a somewhat more logical thing..

"Pani..paniii.."

Suraj still seems to have some courage left in his body and he sees a mirage at a distance, and decides to go into that direction taking the shining liquid for water. He helps her get upright and makes her sit leaning against the sitting camel and starts struggling through the hot sand in the direction of hope. After a while she feels water being sprinkled on her face, bringing her back to life and when she opens her eyes she sees Suraj in a hazy image holding his shoe in his hand. It looks like he is offering her his shoe.

Taking a closer look, she sees that there is water in his shoe and he is trying to get her to drink from it. Disgusted by this gesture she snatches the shoe from his hand and throws it back at his face, it hits Suraj on his head and all the water pours down his exhausted face, she shouts *"SALEY!! I know this is just a dream! Coz it's NIIKE AIR! You JUST CANNOT AFFORD IT!!"*

Then she goes ahead and takes out two cans of Redbul from her sling bag, gives one to the camel and climbs on to it drinking leisurely from the other one, trudging forward leaving the poor guy behind on his knees.

SECOND DATE?

Sneh was sound asleep, exhausted from the long day of birthday bashes and the treacherous room-hunting for her friend. And her damn phone rang, messing with her beauty sleep. She put in maximum effort to grab the phone, hardly opened one of her eyes to look at who dared to ruin her Sunday morning bliss. Reading the name, comfortably pushed the red ignore button. Yes, it was the new guy in her life again. Hardly a minute had passed when the phone rang again, but luckily this time it was just a message bleep, which is way too easy to ignore.

At 12:15 she woke up with Irfan Khan eyes and a groggy attitude, as always. Her body had had its required hours of sleep, as she had a theory which states that the body has no fixed duration of requisite sleep, but it's till the time it wakes itself up without any help from a pestering mother, an irritating servant or an alarm clock. Now she is up, rather just upright on her bed, stretching her arms and her mouth to the maximum. Habitually, she picked up her phone and noticed 2 missed calls and 1 message, all from Suraj. She read the SMS which seems like written in foreign language says *"Kal jo hua tha 7000..lekin 5000 ij ok"*. She did not have a clue what he is talking about and made an ugly face thinking she will have to initiate to call him now because probably it had something to do with her friend's rented apartment.

So she called Suraj. After having to bear the same shitty song for 30 seconds, he picked up. She goes: Hello

Suraj (excited): Hello, *haan..ji kal jo 7000 ka baat hua tha naa.. wo 5000 mein maan jaega, maine malik ko baat karte suna tou bol rye the, 4th floor koi ni le raha hai, tou 5000 pe bhi koi le to dedena. Tou aap 5000 se jyada mat dena, theek hai?"*

After his long proud explanation about his great deed, he was expecting a rather appreciating reply and a word or two praising him, but all he got was a sleepy *"Ok, chal aate hain thodi der mein."* and she dropped back on her most loved furniture.

After the deal was fixed on the leaked prize, Suraj, Sneh and her friend were all at the room as a few things still needed to be taken care of. Sneh's friend was very happy with the deal as this 2000 rupees saved per month mattered a lot to her. They meant more colourful shorts, sandals and beer. She got all overwhelmed and started thanking Sneh repeatedly for this perfect room and offered her a lunch treat. In the heat of the moment and of top-floor room with no air-conditioning, Sneh blurted out "It's all because of him, you should give him a treat" hardly realizing that it totally made sense and might actually materialize!

So they headed out to an Indian restaurant "Odupi", thankfully not berkos this time. Now this restaurant was almost as flashy as berkos if not more and this outing was only the second one for Suraj, but he was feeling more confident this time around, as he was the sole reason for this treat and not an accused of lechery. As all three of them read the menu, suddenly two voices ordered the same thing in different tones.. *"GgOoLlGgAaPpPpEe!"*, and then sunk back in their chairs feeling rather awkward at the same selection.

While enjoying their *gol gappe*, Suraj's thought process took him back to the first day he saw her with same visuals he realized that he is now closer to her. He wondered if it's just the literal distance or have they come closer on other terms as well? He went through their short journey so far, and felt that they might be destined to be together for a longer journey, or maybe just having *gol gappe* together for this first and last time!

Throughout the treat, both the girls kept asking him meaningless questions with their mouths full, like *"Delhi mein kab se ho?"*, *"Tumhara gaon kounsa hai?"* *"Is properties wale ke pass kabse kaam karr rahe ho?"* And Suraj

CHOMP!
CHOMP!

politely answered all their questions without asking anything about them. After the treat, her friend takes a rickshaw to her previous accommodation to pack as it was impossible for Sneh's car to go through the narrow lanes of her colony, especially with Sneh driving.

Suraj being extra generous decided to go to the new apartment to do a last minute check and fix whatever needed to be done to make it comfortable for living. On reaching Sneh's car, he was about to open the rear door, when Sneh interrupted and asked him to take the front seat, saying *"Oye, nahi! Peeche nahi aage baith, nahi tou log kahenge driver piiche baitha hai aur bandi khud chala rahi hai!"* Though derogatory, what she said did not matter to him at all. What mattered was that he is sitting right next to her like a friend, but soon he realized that the 2 lunches he had with her were results of some uncanny circumstances and just sitting next to her does not make him her friend.

Realizing that this was probably the last time he is in a car right next to her, and aware, rather relieved of the fact that she cannot slap him driving with 80% of her conscience involved, he dared to ask her..

"Hum dost kyun nahi ban sakte?"

Instead of going mad like she did during most of her previous encounters with this guy, this time she smiled. And continued to smile, and spoke up *"Hah!..beta guts bohot hain tere mein!"*

Suraj: *Guts? Matlub?*

Sneh (still smiling): Guts ka actual matlub tou nahi..umm.. matlub.. ba.. (she was about to say balls but realized that it would only complicate things for her, so she tried to explain it in Hindi instead) ..*Matlub ..“Nidarta” nidarta* to do anything.

Suraj was still confused as he didn't get what she was implying. So he asked: *Mere pass paisa nahi hai, sirf ye reason tou nahi ho sakta, aapke koi tou friend honge jo aapki tarah paise wale na hon?*

Sneh: *Kya karoge mera friend banke? Shehar ki ladrkiya achi nahi hoti.. bech ke kha jaengi tujhe!*

She didn't give him a straight forward answer but the question did ring in her head for a while and she found that all the reasons were kind of rude or just plain racist, like we cannot be friends because you are poor or you are not from Delhi, she actually tried to figure out some other genuine reasons which can be deemed logical to prevent them from becoming friends.. but strangely enough, she couldn't find any.

Suraj was smart enough to realize that she does not want to answer that, so he sat there quietly till they reach the apartment, and got off her car exchanging some awkward good-byes.

SUNDAY BIZARRE

It's New Year's Eve. A lot has changed for both of them within these two months. Suraj has learned a bit more about Delhi, his *"kario, mariyo, katt gayi, fatt gayi, le lii, de lii"* Delhi slang got even better. He even figured out that the ridiculous horn blowing drivers are actually premature ejaculators! (no control over physical emotions), still no luck to find about the *"baap"* in *"tu jaanta nahi mera baap koun hai"* though.

It was rather amusing for him to notice a common pattern among all Delhiites, they pretend that they are the most carefree fun creatures in the world, but are most paranoid and insecure from the inside. Unfortunate or fortunate for him, all he could know about Delhi was from the roads, as he was never really welcome to the indoors. The only time he would spend inside someone's house would be only for some blue-collar business and under accusing surveillance.

Apart from gaining all this *gyan* about Delhi, he also has gained some confidence and some weight. Sneh too has gained some weight, rather everyone in Delhi has gained some weight, and the weather now is *"tadrpaye tarsaye re" wali Dilli ki sardi!*

Sneh's family had a *"khaandani"* self-made tradition of making Gajrela i.e. *Gajar ka halwa* (read desi ghee laden sweet dish made of carrots) on New Year's Eve and having it the first thing after the new year countdown which they would watch simultaneously on all TV channels, tucked in their quilts. Every Indian festival is about eating sweets anyway. But the problem this year is that their man-Friday *"Chhotu"* had gone back to his hometown and Sneh's dad was on a business tour. Now this left Sneh, high & dry filling in for her dad's and Chhotu's work, as her mother was already busy doing other motherly duties.

Before going on this monstrous "buy veggies-pay cash-take return amount back" mission :p, she diligently made a list of 5 vegetables she needed to get from the market as she can never memorize more than three different things at a time. She reached the market but it was much more difficult than she had thought. She felt like she has landed on Pandora from the movie Avatar, with so many things she was seeing for the first time. Forget knowing their names, she doubted if she had even seen them before, though she was sure she might have eaten most of them but had never cared to find out how they looked before they were cooked. Under all the traffic, noise and hodgepodge, she spotted the most important vegetable for the event, the carrots, lying in a neatly arranged heap. She shoved and pushed past haggling aunties and touchy-feely uncles, and got bumped by a fat aunt's rear-end almost falling on the carrots, but somehow composed herself and shouted several times to get the vendor's attention: *Bhaiya kitne ki di gajar?*

Bhaiya: Hanji?

She: *Ek gajar kitne ki di?*

Bhaiya: (trying to control his smile, realizing that this is her first trip to sabji-land): 25 *rupaye* (he said in a lower voice, hoping that only she would hear and not the overqualified aunties for the occasion)

Having seen other aunties bargaining, she confidently says: *Theek theek lagalo bhaiya.*

Bhaiya: *Chalo theek hai 22 ki ek lelo.*

She (grinning inside like a proud wild fox): *Theek hai 10 pack kardo.*

While making the necessary purchases, she also started looking at other vendors who were not selling vegetables but other things like artificial jewellary, crockery (she had seen almost the same stuff at the home

Tamator Das ka
Sabke Bas ka !!
kya loge?
mydom ji
puchchchhh
naaspiti lele!
tamatar lo!
degi mirch
ka tarka
anng anng
fadrka!!
kaddu hoga tera baap!

section of a mall at triple the prices), second hand clothes (mostly with Christmas prints and Will Smith's jackets from "The Fresh Prince of Bel-Air" days), and a pirated DVD stall. She saw DVDs with covers having low quality prints from movies which have released recently. She was unable to get the tickets back then, so she decided to ask the price. As soon as she raised her hand to get the seller's attention she saw a happy face looking up at her, the sparkle in his eyes is same as the one you see when you scratch the butt of a street dog, who has never had his butt scratched.

It was Suraj, although not a friend, but since otherwise the place felt a little hostile to her cocooned upbringing, she felt a bit relieved and happy on finding a familiar place in this maddening crowd.

Sneh: *Tu yahan kya kar raha hai?*

Suraj: Business! :)

Sneh: *Kyu, properties ka kya hua?*

Suraj: *Wo bhi karta hun, ye bus Sundays ko.*

Sneh: *Oh achcha. Chal ye movie dede..chalegi na?*

Suraj: *Haan haan..maine khud dekhi hai kal.*

Sneh: *Tera number wohi hai? Agar nahi chali tou ghar se wapis leke jaio.*

Suraj: *Theek hai. Aur aap theek ho? Yahan kese? Wo room sahi chal raha hai?*

Sneh: *Aaa?..kya?* (trying to figure what he is saying) Haan.. I guess..*Kyun girne wala tha kya?* (she smiled)

He smiled.

He refused to take money for the DVD but she forced him saying *"Chup be!..Rakhle chup chap!"*

He asked her if she needs any help buying the vegetables but she said she will manage. And she did manage! She reached home to her happy and proud mom as she saved their family's "*Gajar ka halwa* on new year's eve" tradition. Thankfully her mom didn't ask how much she spent!

Even though her friends keep calling her to party with them, but she did not go, as she had this pact with her parents to spend all the festivals with them only, alongside thinking that with her friends, everyday seems like a festival anyway.

10.. 9.. 8.. 7.. 6.. 5.. 4.. 3.. 2.. 1.. *BhushhHH!!!!* It's New Years!!

Wuhuuuuuu!!!!.. *Gajrella!!!* Yawwwnnnhhhh.... Zzzzzzz

On the first day of next year, when she and her mom were enjoying their *Gajar ka halwa* for the second time, she decided to watch the movie she brought yesterday. There is anyhow nothing better to do on college breaks, than to snuggle up in a cozy quilt and enjoy hot sweets and savouries, thanks to the chilling January cold outside. She took out the DVD from its tacky packing and slipped it into the DVD player struggling with one hand, the other holding the bowl with the warm Gajrela, half body hanging from the bed and a spoon clenched in her teeth. Just as the movie began, her cheeks turned to pink and then red and she got totally frustrated finding that it's a cam print.

Cam print, as we all know, where a random guy with a camera bribes the usher at some cinema to let him record the movie on his camera which is all shaky, hazy, out of focus, going haywire many times through the movie, also covering people moving in and out of their seats for loo breaks and refreshments, and babies crying in the background, all in all a shit of an idea!

FUCKIN crap print

Looking like every bit of the lead Angry Bird, she dialled Suraj's number, and even before giving him some time for pleasantries, lashed out at him saying: *Ye kya diya hai tune?* All crap print?

Suraj: *Krap?*

Sneh: *Matlub bilkul kharaab print hai ye.. Tune kaha tha ekdum sahi chalegi?*

Suraj: *Woh nayi movie hai na tou..pehle tou aisa hee print hota hai, phir thoda clear aur bohot mahino baad jaake ekdum clear print ata hai.*

Sneh: *Tou mujhe clear print wali hee chahiye*

Suraj: *Tou main aapko HD wali deta hun..purani hongi par ekdum clear.*

Sneh: *Theek hai abhi de ke ja.*

She avoids going out much when her dad is on tour, as her mom feels lonely. They had considered the idea of keeping a pet dog, but Sneh had rejected this idea because a dog means a lot of responsibility, including taking it for early morning walks, which she could not afford as her body needed the required hours of sleep. Also, she would not take shit from anyone even figuratively, let alone literally! Furthermore, her mother, who is the epitome of emotions, might not be able to take the death of her beloved pet, even if it lived the maximum span dogs are supposed to.

Having nothing much to do, they fell asleep watching senseless daily soaps with all that confusing *"kal aapne dekha"* *"aage aap dekhenge"* *"agle hafte"* *"pichhle hafte"* views. And the doorbell rang. Her mother grumbled *"Pata nahi iss time koun agaya"* trying to get out of the pile of her shawl, the blanket and quilt, when Sneh jumped up saying "I know" and rushed to the door. Here he was after a good four hours as he was downloading the movies right then, with just two DVDs in his hand. As soon as he handed them over, she started her discourse: *Ye kya hai? Titanic Hindi mein?*

Aur Rangeela? Tu pagal hai kya?..Ye bakwaas itni purani movies koun dekhega?

Suraj (almost gasps): *Titanic? Bakwas?*

Sneh: *Matlub theek hai but ab tou pata nahi kitni baar dekh li..aur koi nahi hai kya?*

Suraj: *Abhi ye dekhlo, kal aur leke aunga.*

Sneh: *Theek hai* (with a tone of disappointment)

She came up, flipped the DVDs on the table and went back to the bed, because there was no way that she would watch any of those movies.

But.. After 1 hour 11 minutes and 30 seconds they were at the sketching scene where Leonardo draws Kate wearing only a diamond pendant thingy, which forces someone from the family to go for a bathroom break as it gets awkward judged by the Indian family standards. Just as Leonardo opens his bag of pencils and stuff, jerking his head a little too much to adjust his hair, Sneh took a sideward glance at her mom to check if she would be the one to go to the kitchen or washroom to save herself and her daughter from the upcoming embarrassment. But her mom did not look in the mood to budge out of her multi layered comfort, so she herself decided to leave the cozy comfort of her bed and take a washroom break. Just as she swung her leg off the bed fidgeting for her slipper, her mom spoke up *"Beth ja beth ja..koi baat nahi, 15 baar tou dekha hua hai pehle, tune bhi aur maine bhi.. kuch nahi hota.. ab tou wese bhi badi hogai hai tu"*. She was surprised and nervous at the same time at what her mom would say next, as it can never end at *"Ab tou tu badi hogai hai."*

And was she right! As Leonardo keeps scribbling Kate's curves, her mother shoots out: *Tera koi boyfriend hai?*

Sneh: Nahiiiiiiii (bored tone)..*aapka?*

jack, yeh pehne hue meri tasveer banao...
?
"Sirf" yeh pehne hue!

pUChikk
ChUiinnn

Mom (after a thoughtful pause): *Haan..hai na, but business mein he busy rehta hai.. Soch rahi hun chhor dun!*

And they both smiled at each other somehow avoiding Kate's flashing.

Sneh: *Papa shuru se aise hee hain kya?* Business business?

Mom: *Kyun achche nahi lagte tujhe?*

Sneh: *Nahi, achche tou hain, but aapke sath kitna kam time rehte hain.*

Mom: *Beta, duniya mein do hi tarah ke aadmi hote hain..ek tere papa jese.. aur dusre…*

Sneh: *Dusre?*

Mom: *Dusre mujhe kya pata..* (she said with a smile)

Sneh: *Dusre hote hain Leonardo jese.. "If you jump I jump" :p "if you jump I jump" :p* she said in a sarcastic manly voice mimicking Leonardo.

This is what happens when you watch a movie for more than five times and then after 5 years you watch it again. It loses all its emotions and becomes a spoof of itself! Except for Shahrukh's movies, they are just plain spoofs even on first day first show.

The next day, after 20 minutes of few cycles of run-pant-walk-run, Suraj reached Sneh's house with new DVDs tucked in his pants' waist,and rang the doorbell. This was the first time he came to her home when she was not sleeping, but it still was not an appropriate time as she was in the shower and her mom was not at home. Irritated by the incessant rings from Suraj she cut her half an hour shower to around 17 minutes, wore her shorts and sweat shirt and came over to the balcony, and as she bent over the railings, tiny drops from her wet hair fell on the back of Suraj's neck. Suraj, irritated, looked up guessing that it's probably floor cleaning *pochha* water, spit, bird shit or baby pee..but got pleased to see.. Sneh's shining

face with the sun rays making flares through her twinkling wet hair making her face glow with water sprinkling on his face. He was left mesmerized and numb by her beauty, & kept standing there in the rain of her hair for a few seconds even after she had called him up.

When he came upstairs, saw her up close, he realized that it was just a misconception of her beauty, while actually right now without make up, undone hair, and everyday clothes she looked just like any other fair girl. Then he got mesmerized again when he saw her legs!

Even on this chilly winter day, he was sweating a little. He handed her the pack of 8 DVDs bound with a rubber band. She took the bundle and called him inside. He sat there on a sofa as she came back with two glasses in one hand and a 2 litre bottle of Limca. She poured Limca in the glasses and sat in front of him checking what movies he has brought this time.

Sneh: *Ye cover giley giley kyun hein?*

Suraj: *Wo laane se pehle thoda pani gir gya tha* (though he knew it was his sweat). She noticed that there is Avatar, Transformers, Romeo and Juliet (in Hindi) and some other Bollywood movies. He repeatedly tried not to look at her legs but failed miserably.

She was partially happy with the collection this time, and poured him another glass of Limca even when he said no. She went into her room and returned with her purse asking him the price for the DVDs. He resisted and got up to leave, but she stopped him saying *"Kyun, bohot rahees hai kya tu?"* He smiled and accepted the money, and was about to turn around and walk out, when she took her hand out of her warm pocket and extended it for a handshake. Now this handshake was THE moment! It felt like umm.. umm...... ....scribble........................... scribble.......................scribble.................................

It cannot be described in words, all I can say is that it felt way better to Suraj than what this same hand felt on his face a few months ago. It was special. If this story ever gets adapted into a movie, this handshake would be in ultra slow motion, for about 37 seconds, it will be the longest handshake in the history of Bollywood.. with every detail of a handshake like hands raising, fingers opening and clutching the other hand, a subtle squeeze and the synchronized bobbling movement of two hands as if they belong to a single person.

As he left, she waited on the balcony to see if he is closing the gate as told to, which he did, and there was another goodbye, this time without any hand gestures.

After that day, she and her mother watched many movies, not in the way diligent film makers would want them to.. Her mom cooked between them, she slept through many parts, Sneh making funny comments all through, laughing at the funny parts and more at the sad ones, talking rubbish about all the cheesy Bollywood theories and having a really good time.

Then one day when they were watching "Transformers", Sneh's inside voice suddenly spoke up "Why the hell does the hero have to be broke ass poor in every fucking film!!"

It was just a thought..but then she realized and started to wonder about what every movie was about, irrespective of Bollywood or Hollywood. Starting from Titanic to Rangeela, to Transformers..every movie was about a poor guy rich girl falling in love, except for Avatar, which too kind of featured an inter caste relationship. It's a trap! She concluded.

This made her feel how stupid and weird is this guy that he created a collection of movies that have poor-rich relationship, just to make her think that it's possible between them, and she also found it kind of cute that he has no idea of what real life is all about.

ISHTHA CHATTERJEE KI NAYI PESHKASH
THE HANDSHAKE
STARRING SNEH & SURAJ

RHETORICAL QUESTION

It was 4 pm, Suraj was busy setting up his stall at the Sunday bazaar, all he had to do is open his folding table, spread the CDs out of his bag, plug in a tiny cheap DVD player, hang a light bulb which has a red paper wrapped over it to get some DEV D effect going and it is done. As soon as his stall was set up, it would start attracting customers, as the tantalizing *adh-nangi* Bollywood heroines are definitely more interesting than the mounds of onions, tomatoes, potatoes and cheap plastic toiletries being sold alongside. Most people would ask random questions regarding the picture quality, price etc., all the while picking up the CDs in their hands and feasting through their eyes. Still to make his first sale of the day, he sat idle, with both hands in pockets shaking his legs with boredom and cold.

Suddenly he felt a tap on his shoulder, and he turned around to see Sneh standing there with a poker face. On the other hand Suraj is grinning like a Cheshire cat. Sneh gestured to call him at a distance from his stall & says: *Ye le ye teri CDs hain saari. Maine tou dekh li hain mujhe nahi chahiye. Tu dubara bech liyo.* (keeping her voice low)

Suraj: Theek h..

Sneh further added interrupting him (still keeping her voice low): *Aur sunn.. mere pe chance maarna chhor de! Kis umeed mein hai bhai tu?*

Suraj: *Maine kya kiya?*

Sneh: *Nahi, kuch nahi kiya..main bus tujhe bta rahi hun, hum friend frunnd nahi ban sakte aur mujhe ab koi movies bhi nahi chahiye ok.*

Suraj: *Kyun?* (he was actually trying to ask her why she does not want more movies from him) But Sneh thought that he is asking why they can't be friends.

Sneh: *Dekh hum alag hain bhai!* (using this B word with a little too much stress, for it to get stuck in Suraj's head)

Tu banda sahi hai, I have nothing against you, but *tu mere pichhe kyun pada hai? Aur koi nahi mili kya tujhe? Mere mein aisa kya khaas hai jo tu itna pagal hue jara hai bhai?! Accha bataa kya karega mera friend banke, kya baat karenge hum? Na tu college mein hai, na Delhi ka hai. Bhasha bhi teri mujhe mushkil se samaj ati hai..kya karenge friend banke bta?*

It was a rhetorical question, but Suraj did not know of any such thing, so he replied: *Movie dekh sakte hain!*

Sneh (sighed and opened her eyes after taking a deep breath): *Abe ameer gareeb, inter-caste love story type movie dekhne se kuch nahi hota! Real life alag hoti hai, tu kounse gaon se aya hai yaar..aaj-kal tou gao mein bhi..*

Suraj (interrupting her): *Nahi aisa kuch nahi hai 'Kal Ho Na Ho' mein.*

Sneh: *Kal Ho Na Ho?*

Suraj: *Haan, mere paas 2 tickets hain aaj shaam ki..*

Sneh: *Wo tou parson hee release hui hai, tujhe kahan se mil gyi?*

Suraj: *Wo maine bohot din pehle hee leli thi, mera dost bimaar hai tou main akela kya dekhunga.*

Sneh: *Nahi mujhe nahi dekhni hai.* Thanks!

Suraj: *Aapko mere saath nahi jaana tou mat jao. Dono tickets lelo.*

Sneh: *Koun se hall ki hain?*

Suraj: *PVR ki hain..Shahrukh ki picture main kisi aise wese hall pe nahi dekhta!*

Sneh (cringing and smirking on his overly Shahrukh-obsessed behavior) says: *Ek shart pe dekh sakte hain.. Tu kisiko bolega nahi! Aur aage bhi hum koi friend nahi honge, bus movie dekh ke bye bye!*

Suraj: *Haan haan theek hai..aap aajana.. main wahan pe hee milunga 6 baje se pehle.*

She made her way back wondering what the hell she was thinking, why can't she just wait and watch that movie with her real friends! Maybe it was not about the movie, maybe she actually wanted to be his friend but was somehow stopping herself, maybe she liked the sense of adventure she gets whenever he says something to her, maybe she just likes being stupid. Then she thought about all the negatives, like what if he is a criminal psychopath, just pretending to be harmless. But she negates this thought after mentally estimating his wrist size and wondering if he could rape her.

On the other hand Suraj asked his bazaar colleague friend: *Bhai jo tu tickets laya tha hamare liye, wo mujhe dede, taaki main apni friend ke saath chala jaun..tere sath dubara baad mein dekh lunga.*

But his friend gave him a shocked look: *Ticket? Kounsi ticket? Ticket tou mili hee nahi thi!*

Suraj: *Abe saale tuune tou kaha tha aage ki seat ki mili hein!*

Friend: *Tera sada hua chini phone badal le! Maine kaha tha ki bilkul aage ki mil rahi thi, isliye maine nahi li.*

Suraj: *Abe yaaaaaaar!!*

Run- pant-walk-brisk...

Suraj was now at the cinema ticket window, where there is hardly any crowd. He joined the small queue of 7-8 people ahead of him listening to what the ticket guy is saying about the tickets. When the first guy asked about KHNH tickets, he clearly said *'house full hai'*. The remaining 7 people behind the first guy started leaving the ticket window with their heads hung low like they were about to be beheaded by their terrorist wives and girlfriends.

Suraj, the brave-heart, the ever-optimistic still went ahead and asked for tickets. The counter guy just shook his head & refused, to which Suraj again asked *"Bhai saab koi jugaad nahi ho sakta kya?"*

Ticket guy: *Nahi..kuch nahi ho sakta!*

Suraj sat there with a sad face waiting to be embarrassed and probably never having a chance like that again. It was 20 minutes to 6 and people started to come in for the show. Within 10 minutes the queue was up to more than 15 people. Boys, girls, families, all eagerly waiting to enjoy the emotional extravagance of King Khan. At the end of the queue he saw two chirpy 20 plus girls in shorts and skimpy tops, with their boyfriends, one of whom is asking one of the boys to get something to eat, whilst he was trying to persuade her that the movie would start soon and they don't have enough time. But she doesn't care, and throws a fit which is supposed to be cute but looks rather annoying. Finally both the guys left to get something from the nearby kathi roll shop. Suraj was amazed how such girls can make boys go so crazy that they end up fulfilling all their whims and fancies!

With this thought, he came up with a plan, stood up from the pavement and walked slowly towards the girls and with an innocent face he said *"Didi, aap mujhe please do tickets le doge? Mujhe English nahi aati aur wo ticket wala kuch kuch puche ja raha hai, wo kehra hai ki hain ticket but aur bhi kuch bataana parega"*. The girl he asked was a bit flabbergasted but the other one said *"le dete hain yaar"*. The girls went up to the window

TICKET
ahe he..
enjoy yur show

and came back with two tickets as smooth as power puff girls coming back from their world-saving mission. Even Suraj was surprised that his half hearted plan worked like that! He had no idea that every cinema hall keeps a stock of tickets reserved for some special people..

..and no one is more special than girls in skimpy tops! ;)

Now the smile was back on his face as he waited for his "not friend", wondering if she would be wearing anything like the girls who bought him tickets. He saw her walking into the mall, got checked by security and then escalator after escalator till she reached the top floor. He straightens up his back, finger combs his hair and strikes the most stylishly lame pose.. resting his elbow on the railing with one hand holding the other.

Sneh, looking at her watch, ignored all his sex appeal.. *"Chalein"* she said with half a smile, they got inside and took their seats as the screen showed the anti-smoking cancer campaign, which was kind of relevant as King Khan is a chain smoker in real life and does die in the movie.

KAL NA HO TOU NA SAHI

During the first half of the movie, they both shared smiles, laughter, raised eyebrows, disgusted looks, frowns..but all with the characters on the big screen, nothing in between them. They were staring at the screen like complete strangers, not even a single word! Suraj kept looking at her from time to time hoping all the while for her to say something to him, but she was totally lost in the movie. During the interval, when the theatre lights turned on, she finally peeled her eyes off the screen and looked at him, asking: *Kaisi lag rahi hai?*

Suraj: *Theek hai..abhi tak tou.*

Sneh: *Hmmm, chal kuch le ke aate hain.*

They reached the crowded snack counter, where she joined the queue for snacks, and was about to take out her little pouch, when he stopped her. *"Main deta hun"* he said.

Sneh: *Nahi! Tune tickets li na, main de ryi hun, bol kya lena hai?*

She ordered a bucket full of popcorn, a large cola, nachos and a hot dog. Suraj went for a small cola and small popcorn. He just could not muster the courage to order more looking at the price even after knowing that she was paying.

She realized that she must go to the washroom to spend the second half of the movie in peace. She handed the cash over to Suraj and rushed towards the washroom. Among all this ruckus, Suraj was handed his tray full of all their goodies, but before he could have grabbed hold of it, the counter guy let go!

Wham! ThiShhh!! SplaSh!! PaChakkkk!!!

The tray dropped right on the floor, with cola splattered all over and popcorn & nachos floating in it.

The counter guy seemed to be in an all sorry mode but as soon as he realized that the customer does not seem to have a strong social or physical status, he tried to overpower him and refused to give him a repeat of his order, blaming it all on him. Suraj might have looked frail, but knew when and how to stand up for himself! So he refused to budge from next to the cash register and claimed a repeat, stating the carelessness of the counter guy.

Other people in the queue started to crib, fearing they would miss the stupendous death of King Khan on screen! (I've used the word "stupendous" as it kind of sounds like it means stupid :p)

The counter guy in return took it all out on Suraj and pushed his shoulder to remove him from the cash register and serve others.

Now Suraj completely lost his calm and shouted

"HAATH MAT LAGAA DIO!"

Counter guy: *Kyun, kya kar lega bey!... SAALE BIHARI!!*

It was this particular moment which changed Suraj and Sneh's life forever.

She was still a good 20 feet away from the scene, but listening to this word 'Bihari' somehow made her feel it has got to be related to her. She came rushing through the crowd in between Suraj and the cash machine, without asking anything, pushed Suraj away and grabbed and pulled the counter guy by his collar, grinning her teeth & shouting:

"BIHARI KISKO BOLA BE? HAIN? HAAN HAIN HUM BIHARI..TOU? SAALE KHUD YAHAN FULLE BECH RAHA HAI, POCCHE MAAR RAHA HAI AUR HAMEIN NEECHA DIKHANE KI KOSHISH KAR RAHA HAI? APNA BUSINESS HAI HAMARA! MOVIES KA! TERI TARAH YAHAN LOGON KI TATTIYAN NAHI UTHA RAHE JO TU KUCH BHI BOLDEGA HAMEIN! MANAGER KAHAN HAI TERA BULA ABHI!"

The counter guy went numb, which was a good idea for him as he would have gotten slapped had he said anything more.

She asked Suraj..*Hua kya?*

He told her that he dropped our tray.

Sneh (again): *Manager kahan hai?*

Manager had actually been right there, trying to hide behind his crew, hoping he does not have to be involved. But that didn't happen.

He eventually appeared saying "Please calm down ma'am, we are extremely sorry, we'll get your order to your seat."

She took a deep breath as they walked back to the hall quietly

Suraj asked her (with a straight face): Tattiyan bhi yehi uthate hain kya?

She (laughed a little on herself): Kyun? Tune uthani hai? Puchlio job ke liye..

Tatti*

For some reason this disgusting word got stuck in Suraj's head and made him feel so very good. He felt like she is not the queen that she always seems to be, the girl whom he can never think of befriending, but this word, this filthy little word made him feel extremely close to her, as he

SOb!
SOb!

himself uses this word an awful lot of times at home and with friends . If not already, he has fallen in love with her now, the way she took his side and called herself a Bihari, for a while it kind of felt like they were already married.

Plus this outburst had broken all the ice between them that seemed impossible to break earlier. Now they were talking between scenes, she started making funny comments on all the mushy and sad dialogues as she would do at home with her mom, but this time she was on the receiving end as well, as Suraj would reply to her comments and make further comments, even more weird.

In the scene where Shahrukh is giving away his love to Saif before dying, a lady sitting behind their row kept saying *'hawww..bichara..'*, and they could not control themselves anymore. They burst out laughing so loud that the torch guy had to come up to them and request them to keep it low (like they were going to listen).One joke after another, laughter and more laughter, and they ruined the movie for about 6-7 seats in all 4 directions. For a moment she forgot that she was with someone who is not even her friend.

After the movie, when they were going down the stairs, people were giving them dirty looks like they were coming out of their own shitty movie premiere. She asked him to come with her, that she would drop him. While they were in her car, they were almost going back to their "not friend" stranger zone, but she broke the silence and said: *hum friend ban sakte hain. Matlub try tou kar hi sakte hain at least! But ek shart pe.. Tumhe bina kuch question kiye..*

..mera sara kehna manna parega.. matlub kuch time tak!

He had no words for it, just imaginary fireworks, rainbows and arrows piercing through hearts in the sky and a huge wolfish grin on his face, which got wider when she said *"Kal milte hain? 11baje?"*

aaj main uuper ..

JUST DO IT

Next morning, 11:45 am. She parked her car, found him standing there waiting for her, analyzing people like a pedophile outside a kids school. She was late by 45 minutes, but he greeted her with a nonchalant smile, as if she was 45 minutes ahead of time. As she said 'Hi', she noticed that instead of looking at her face he was pointing towards his shirt's collar in an uncomfortable way all the while clearing his throat going 'ahem ahem'. She asked him what the matter is, unable to gauge the meaning of his weird gestures but he continued till she realized that he was pointing at her top's unbuttoned top button.

Sneh: *Abe ye fashion hai..tu upar dekh na!*

They walked in the market for a while when she stopped outside the Niike showroom. Suraj wondered if the sole reason for this whole exercise is that he is supposed to hold her shopping bags while she shops. She went through the racks of clothing while he stood there staring at the Nadal poster pumping his fist in a victorious stance. While Suraj was admiring Nadal's muscular body, Sneh came over from behind him and put a red T-shirt on his shoulders to see whether it is his size. He was rather surprised at this and asked her what she was trying to do.

Sneh: I am buying you some clothes. *Tumhare liye gift!*

Suraj: *Kyun? Aaj mera birthday thodi hai!*

Sneh: *Chup!* No questions..remember?

Sneh would speak half of her sentences in English out of habit, but he understood most of it, by picking up words and also by her gestures &

expressions. In fact he had started using a few English words himself.

Sneh continues: *"Tune wo kahaawat nahi suni, jab Delhi mein raho tou Delhi walon jaisa banke raho?"* She just copy pasted the 'When in Rome do as the Romans do' thing on Delhi.

He went into the trial room and emerged wearing the red T-shirt with the Niike logo and the slogan 'Just Do It' inscribed under it. Sneh got totally amazed by how he still looked as uncool as before, if not more, in that cool T-shirt. But she did not lose hope, and expected him to look better after having been given a complete makeover.

Now she went around looking for some nice shoes for him that might make him look a bit taller than her. She picked up basketball Jordan shoes worth Rs.6000 and asked Suraj to remove his V-shaped hawai chappal. But the sales guy interrupted him saying "Sorry sir, you cannot try these". Sneh got back in her angry young woman mode as she grits her teeth saying "Why the fuck not?"

The sales guy did not say anything & kept looking down, so Sneh followed his point of view, found Suraj's feet, and the words "Oh God" just flew out of her mouth! He had the most hideous pair of feet, with dirt stuck in all nooks and corners and a permanent black inverted V-mark from the slipper straps. She sincerely apologized to the sales guy and saying that they would be back in a while, dragged him out.

They rushed out of the showroom and Sneh almost shouted out: *Kya hai ye, itne gande peyr?*

Suraj: *Wo subah cricket khelne gya tha na...*

Sneh: *Chup reh! Ek din ke nahi hain ye! Ab kya karein?*

Suraj told her that there is a hand pump close by. They got there, she stood mute, and saw as Suraj folded his pants up to his knees, pump the lever,

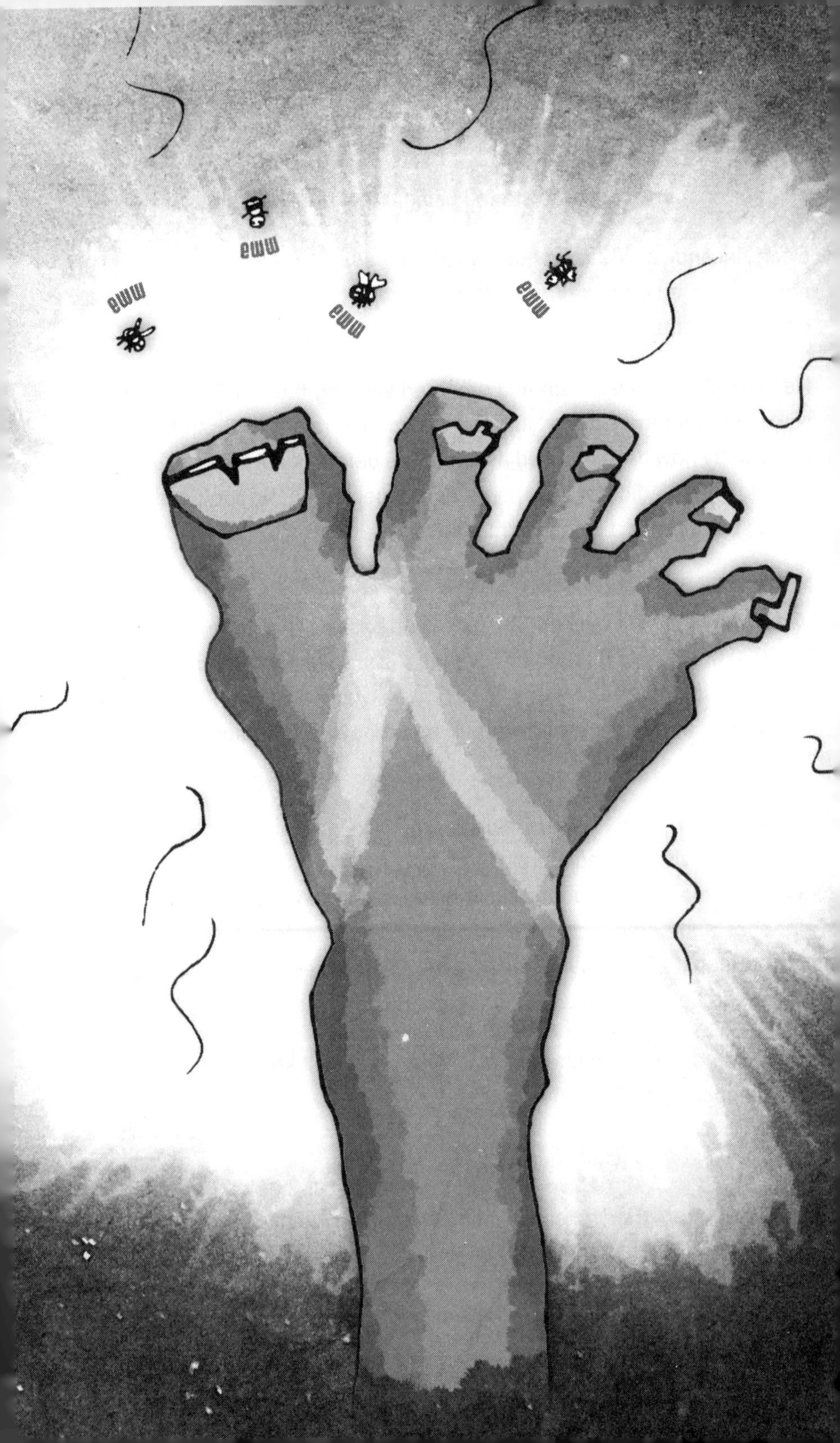
eww
eww
eww
eww

but by the time he got around to put his feet under the flowing water, it lost the flow pressure & his feet were too dirty to get cleaned by that trickle of water. She rolled her eyes and realized that this makeover mission is not going to be easy! She purchased a bar of Dov soap from the nearby chemist and handed it to Suraj. Now she was pumping the lever while he was cleaning his feet thoroughly, to prevent any further embarrassment. She felt so empowered, so independent about doing this deed that she got carried away and pumped away to glory, really hard! And at one point the lever went down..Hac!! Cramp!! Ouch!! She ended up getting sprained, and now cannot even straighten up her back. Suraj leaves his soap and rushes to get her upright but she shouts out 'Do not touch me!' which he clearly understands just by the tone, no knowledge of English language required here. He backs off and looks around how to help her, when she shouts again 'Ok fine, just do it!' He puts his soapy hand on her lower back and the other on her shoulder, cranks her body up and she stands after much struggling and wincing in pain. She says a sarcastic 'Thank you' for putting her in such a situation, and he ignorantly says 'Welcome'.

He cleaned off the remaining soap from his feet and is rather surprised to see that his feet are actually not black in colour, rather they are quite fair, probably because they have always had a layer of "*maiyl*" over them.

They went back to the Niike store, where he was now allowed to try on the shoes, amidst murmurs from the other sales staff. Sneh hears them saying stuff like "why would she be doing so much for a guy like him... maybe he saved her life (giggles)", but she did not react and ignored them completely. She was now getting used to all this and realized that she cannot go around fighting all the racist Delhiites. In fact these incidents somehow got her closer to him.

So after much negation on her buying him such expensive stuff, and her not listening to his whining, here he was, wearing black basketball shoes and shorts with ankle length socks and a red T-shirt. Sneh had a sporty

tough guy look in her mind, but all that came out of this eventful day was a guy who looked like the 7Up mascot, Fido Dido if you remember, sans the spikey wavy hair. He still had the '*Raju ban gaya gentleman*' SRK hairstyle.

They ended up buying 4 T-shirts, two pairs of shorts, 3 pairs of track pants, 4 pairs of socks, Jordan shoes and a backpack to carry all that.

Coming out of the showroom, Suraj asked her about the T-shirt he was wearing.

"Ye bana kya hua hai, ispe?"

Sneh: Logo hai, company ka.

Suraj: *Saale Rs.1400 ka T-shirt humne liya aur logo company ka? Itne paise mein tou aage mera aur pichhe meri maa ka naam hona chahiye tha!*

To which she didn't really react, as she was still adjusting her back.

Then putting this makeover task on hold they decided to eat something. As they took their chairs in a small restaurant, she took out a Fair and Lively tube from her purse which had a complexion shade card attached to it. She jokingly put the shade card on his face and smiled: *Abe isme tou tera shade hee nahi hai yaar!*

He just smiled like a monkey. Like this was the best compliment anyone had ever given him.

Sneh continues: *Chal jaldi se kuch khate hain, phir teri cutting bhi karaani hai.*

Suraj: *Kya? Maine nahi karaani koi cutting! Ek tou joker jaise kapde pehna diye, upar se ganja karaana hai ab?*

Sneh: *Kya hai ye gande se purane Shahrukh wale baal? Upar se brown! Oil nahi lagata kya?*

Suraj: *Nahi! Brown ache lagte hain. Titanic ke hero ke bhi tou brown hain!*

Sneh (not trying too hard to suppress her smile): *Saale wo Leonardo hai! ooo, tou tu khud ko Leonardo samajhta hai! Tabhi Titanic load kar ke di thi mujhe?*

Suraj (Blushing with embarrassment): *Nahi..wo tou bas.*

A newlywed couple walked in the restaurant and took the table next to them. The lady is wearing a Punjabi chuuda with a beautiful multicoloured suit. They both checked them out a bit, all this while Suraj hoping that maybe they also get married someday, and smiled a little.

Sneh: *Kya?*

Suraj: *Kuch nahi.*

Sneh: *Beta sapne lele tu! Humari koi shadi wadi nahi hone wali kabhi! Hum bas friend type hain, shadi tou main kisi bohot hee khaas bande se karungi nahi tou karungi hee nahi.*

Suraj: *Khaas matlub? Rassi pe chalne wala? Ya chawal ke dane pe Ramayan likhne wala?*

She makes a frustrated face.

Suraj: *Ooo..matlub bohot paise wala.. jaise Dilli mein kehte hain RAHEES!*

She: *Haan! Ab samjha na tu.*

Suraj: *Rahees ladko mein itna khaas kya hota hai? Bas paisa?*

Sneh: *Hmm.*

Suraj: *Matlub paisa hee sab kuch hota hai zindagi mein?*

Sneh: *Nahi..paisa sab kuch nahi hota, but paise ke bina kuch bhi nahi hota!*

Suraj: *Main jab Delhi aya tha tou main ne ek mahina ek ghar mein kaam kiya tha, ghar ki safai, car saaf, kutte ghumana. Ek uncle aunty the, unke teen bete the..jo sabse bada tha wo bohut harami tha, apni biwi ko maarta tha, roj sharab peeta tha, bahar logon se ladta tha, roj police ka aana jana.*

Usse chhota bohot masti karta tha, roj nayi ladki, nayi nayi gaadiyaan, music, nashe.

Aur usse chhota bus phones, computer, gandi picturein aur games mein ghusa rehta tha.

Un teeno k baad meine jitney bhi ameer ladke dekhe hein, wo in mein se hee ek jaise hote hain, ya teeno ka mix!

Aise kisi se hi shadi karaani hai aapko?

Sneh, bored from his long description said: *Haan, aur kya! Party, nashe, ladkiyan, ladaaiyaan, gadgets..aur kya chahiye life mein mujhe?*

Mid-way their steaming pizzas landed on their table, declaring the end of that discussion.

Looking at his pizza Suraj says: *Oh ye pizza hota hai? Ye tou mere dost ki mummy bhi banati hai ghar mein. Bas uspe sabjiyan thodi jyada hoti hein, aur thoda bada hota hai.*

Sneh did not even respond to his comment and dug into her pizza like she's there alone. During the meal, Suraj made it very clear that he is not going for the haircut, no matter what, and that he would pay the money back for the clothes she had bought him and also for his share of the pizza. So it was only this far Sneh could get about Suraj's makeover.

Later that night, Sneh's mom comes to her room rushing like never before, She was holding her black kurta, with white soapy spots on its lower-back and shoulder, and asked her if she travelled by bus.. to which she replied " no mom, I was sitting under a tree today." Referring to the soapy spots to be bird dropping and not what her mother was thinking!

After this day of his semi make over, they kind of dated for a few months, and met once, twice, sometimes even thrice a week! They got emotionally tuned to each other, all the friends and facebook friends were shocked and against it at first, then they were like "why?" and soon without even getting any justification, everyone seem to be "OK, whatever" with it!. It seems everything in this world comes like a "mohawk"..questioned and ridiculed first, then becomes the most awesome thing, and soon, it's ordinary as shit!

Things were going all happy and smooth, till this long bad day..

LONG BAD DAY

It was just another regular day, no festival, no monthly or half yearly anniversary, no one's birthday but she found Suraj's voice on the phone a little over-excited over something. It was the first time in their relationship, he wanted to see her on that particular day so eagerly and early in the morning and said that he has a surprise for her. She would have never decided to meet him on this specific day as it was "that" time of the month for her, but after his sudden call, suspense and excitement, she thought... "what the heck!"

There he was, smiling like a high rapper in a music video surrounded by paid bitches, wearing one of those full sleeved Niike T-shirts, which she bought for him when they had newly met. She thought that he was still not looking good enough for this to be a surprise for her. As she got closer to him, he raised his hand like a beggar, and before she can ask what is it all about, he pulled the sleeve up to the elbow, revealing a 3"x 1" tattoo that said "Sneh"!

Contrary to what Suraj had thought her reaction would be, she freaked out.

Sneh: Is it permanent? It cannot be permanent! Don't tell me it's permanent ...fuck! It is permanent!..fuck! fuck! fuck!... *tu pagal hai kya?*.. what the..??

Suraj's smile turned into a frown: *Kyun? Kya hua? Acha nahi hai?*

Sneh: *Abhi humara koi future hai bhi ya nahi.. kuch pata nahi.. abhi humein bus 6 mahine hue hain aur.. agar hamara koi scene nahi banta tou kya karega?*

Suraj: *Haan, mujhe pata hai, humara future nahi ho shayad, par ye sirf abhi ke liye hai, chahe koi future ho ya na ho, ye bus in 6 mahino ke liye hai jo main kabhi nahi bhulunga.*

Sneh: *Jab bhulega nahi tou phir tattoo karane ki kya jarurat thi? Dard nahi hua?*

Suraj made a face that seemed to be totally inspired by Shahrukh's and said: *Itna tou nahi, jitna ab ho raha hai!*

She had no idea what he meant by that but as soon as she realized she guffawed which even made Suraj smile and they went ahead with their date.

They decided to go to Connaught Placc (an open market now named Rajiv Chowk) as the weather was cloudy with cool breeze flowing, which is one of the very few conditions in which Sneh likes to be out in the open. Otherwise 90% of their dates were in air conditioned malls with proximity to clean toilets. During the day, she looked at the tattoo like 52 times, and every time she saw it, she started to feel special and special and thought it could have been a lot worse if he had added an 'I love you' or had a stupid heart with a piercing arrow and their initials over it.

While they were on their way, it started to rain, and after a lot of whining and cribbing about how the drops would ruin her car seats, or how the sticky wind would ruin her hair, she let Suraj roll down his window glass and feel the rain droplets on his arm and face. To which she smiled and said: Are you a dog? I've only seen dogs do that! To which he howled: Auuuooouuuuuu… aaaaauuuooouuuuu & bent towards her to forcefully open her window as well.

And then they stopped their car in the middle of a road, got out and started dancing to "*tan tan tan dran tan tan… tan tan tan. tadran tan tran dan… tip tip barsaa paani..pause.. paani ne aag lagai*".. Ok, sorry, no, that didn't happen, (the song and dance thing) it's just my favourite rain song..but yeah! There was this little spark lit up between them due to the rain.

They spent all their time hopping from shed to shed, still unable to prevent themselves from getting at least 30% soaked in the rain. Soon, they completely surrendered themselves to nature.. and got drenched in the rain like poor little naked kids you see in the next day newspapers after heavy rains. Just when they were about to make their way back to the car parking, Suraj stopped at the poster guy sitting around a pillar with his treasure trove of all kinds of posters imaginable! Most of the posters were of rock bands and football players, so it made Sneh wonder what made Suraj stop.

But as soon as she had started wondering, she saw what his hand was going to pick and she thought-slapped her head. He did pick up a Leonardo DiCaprio & Kate Winslet poster from Titanic in the most romantic pose ever :p, with the caption "Nothing on earth could come between them".

"Oh come on!" she told herself as she couldn't believe his obsession with the movie. When they were on their way home, she kept asking him what it is about the movie that he likes it so much? But he could not come up with an answer.

Sneh: You know what happens to Leo in the end of the movie, right? He dies!

Suraj: *Haan, magar asal zindagi main uski har mahine akhbaar mein nayi ladki ke saath photo aati hai.*

Sneh: *Achcha! tou tujhe Leonardo ban ke har mahine nayi ladki chahiye.. hain? But agar tu hota na movie mein, tou bach jata, cos tera kuch weight hee nahi hai, araam se dono leyt jaate board pe.*

Without letting him react, she further went on guessing the reasons for liking the movie so much:

"It was the first English movie you saw, which you saw in Hindi though?"

"You are gay and have hots for white blonde guys?"

"It was the first time you saw a set of foreign boobs?"

"The steamy sex in the car scene..right?"

Suraj first had his eyes wide open in shock and then he kept laughing with each of her guesses. But the last one left him dumbstruck. He did not say anything, and rather stopped laughing abruptly and put his hand on her thigh. And before she could react, he just leaned in and kissed her under her ear while she was driving.

She did not react much, just kept driving. Now Suraj was not even sure whether she was angry or whether it didn't matter to her at all.

Way to their home was straight and about 15 minutes drive away now, but she slowed down a few blocks behind and took a left turn into a colony that seemed dim lit. It was around 7 pm and most of the streets in this particular colony looked desolate. But as soon as she drove in, they saw that it was bustling with children playing badminton, aunties gossiping, and uncles taking their evening walks. There was hardly any place to park, let alone a secluded place which by now Suraj had realized that they were looking for.

The only thing harder than finding a parking spot in Delhi is to find a parking spot at a dim lit secluded place with no one around to bother. After quietly roaming around with apprehension for about 12 minutes, they found a back lane that seemed perfect to commence their *"ashleel"* program.

They sat upright for a few minutes to make sure that nobody is looking. There was no one around and it was too dark for anyone to notice anyway. She slid back her seat suggestively and leaned on him and he leaned back further as they shared their first kiss, which grew, more and more passionate with each second. All this while, Suraj had his eyes wide open like an owl, and he just kept staring at her face wondering if this was an open-eyed dream. After a few minutes of vigorous lip locking, they lost their senses to someone between cupid of love and the devil of lust.

Putting the seat further down, they got on the back seat, now he was all over her, body on body, breath in breath, eyes locked with mixed expressions of shock, hunger, love, and some traces of guilt too. Now she started hastily unbuttoning his shirt, and he didn't take a moment to remove his shirt as soon as all the buttons were unfastened, and threw it on the front seat.

He helped her get her top off, as they shared their first 'I love you' and many more puffy I love you(s) in the heat of the moment, It all felt like one heavenly moment to them and seemed like a bright light fell on them.. hazily distributed all over through the steam laden windowpanes. It was as if they were about to be abducted by an alien ship! And before they could have realized what was happening in the bright light, the light started to move away. And what dawned upon them was nothing less of an avalanche. It was an Enfield motorbike's headlight, and even in the darkness of this unfortunate night, Suraj could clearly make out that it was yellow in colour. That meant that it was a Delhi Police patrol bike, and they were busted, red-handed! The amazing part was that the bike hardly made a sound to bring them back to reality, because these bikes are meant to declare their arrival from about a quarter kilometer away! Maybe they were too engrossed in their love making session, or maybe the cop was too interested in catching them in a compromising position, and hence had turned his engine off a good mile away and dragged the super heavy bike just to pounce on them with the headlight at the right moment. (Awesome isn't it?! Doesn't he deserve a *Param Veer Chakra* on the 26th January for this!)

Their hormones went down from the verge just like boiling milk does in its pail when the stove is turned off.

All Suraj wanted to do was to get her safe and sound out of the scene, as he had seen the look of horror on her face. He just wanted to get out of the car as quickly as possible, to face the dire consequences of this act himself, so he made a failed attempt at grabbing his shirt, groping and fiddling in the dark car, and just got out of the car as it is, after telling her to just drive away from the scene. It was only a matter of seconds ago that they were having the time of their life, and now here he was, all alone, facing a cop, topless!

The situation had all the colours for him to be mistaken as some meager thief and get beaten up by a mob, but lucky for him that there was no one except the two of them.

Even the cop was rather amused by his semi nude act, so he told him to call her and get his shirt back, and dare not try to run away as he had noted down the car number.

Suraj could tell from this little discussion with the cop that all that he was looking for was a little bribe. So he called her on her phone and asked her to calm down as this matter would be settled with some amount of money. She came back with the car just at the corner of the street, from where he grabbed his shirt and asked her to wait outside the street in a well-lit place.

When Suraj got back to the cop wearing his shirt.

Policeman: *Haan bhai..kya kar rahe the? Chalein thane?*

Suraj: *Nahi sir ji aisa kuch nahi kar rahe the, bas yahin bata do kya ho sakta hai, aage se nahi karenge.*

Policeman: *Nikaal de phir paanch hajaar!*

Suraj (had no words for this bullshit but still couldn't say much except): *Sir kya baat kar rahe ho, bacche hain. Bus ye sou rupaye jeb mein pade hain..Le lo.*

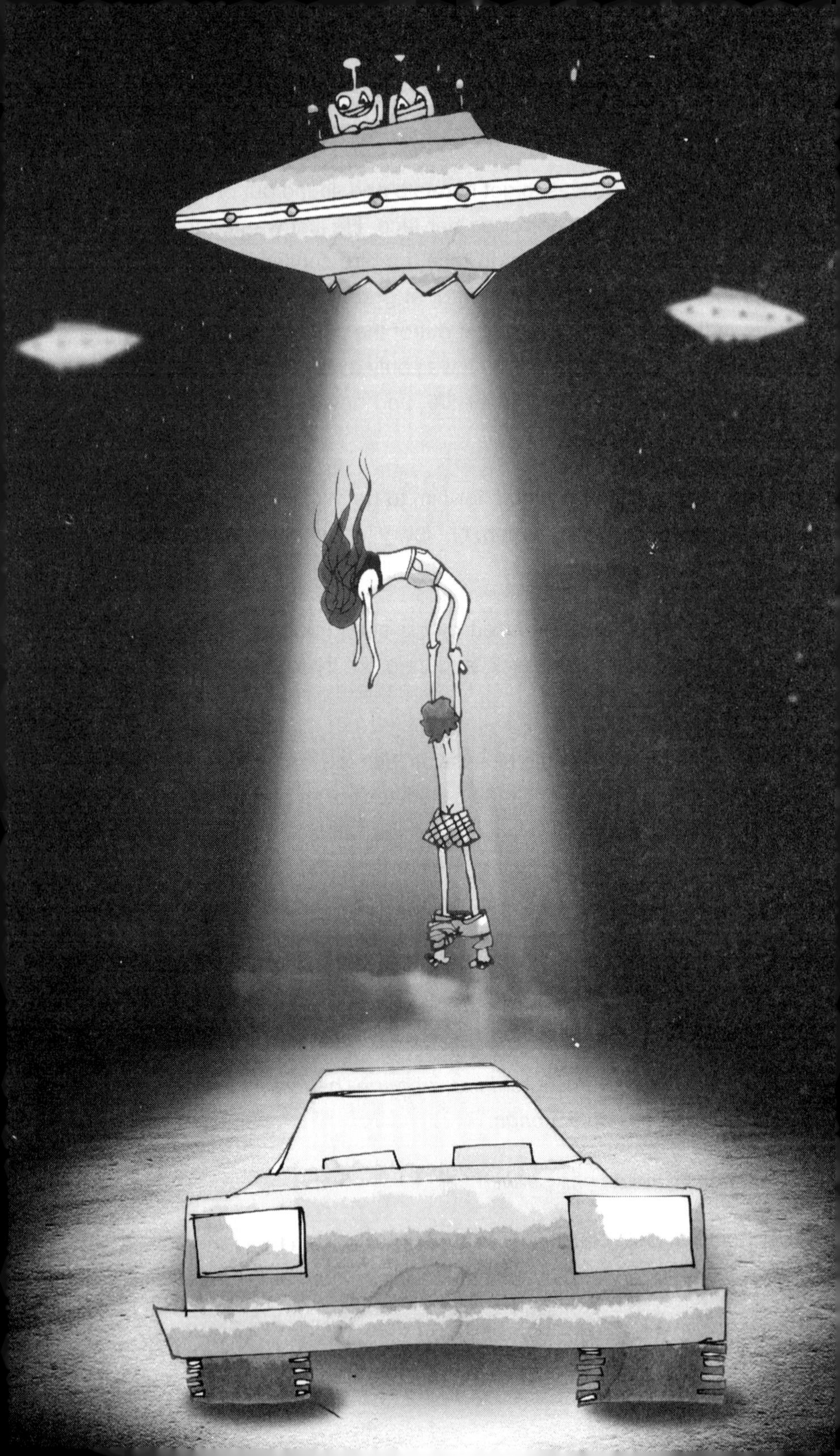

Policeman grabs the 100 rupee note and asks Suraj to get some more from the girl.

Suraj: *Nahi sir ji, Ladki ke paas kuch paise nahi hain, gariib ghar ki hai bechari..bas ye hee bache hain aaj.*

Policeman: *Achha? Chal mera number likh, aur ghar ja ke 500 ka recharge karwa dio.*

Suraj: *Theek hai sir ji.* (Knowing that once he is out of there, they would never see him again)

It was over 9 pm, and there was no way that they were going to try that again, at least not for a few weeks.

Near the red light right next to her colony, they recalled the whole incident and laughed their hearts out, forgetting the stress that they had just gone through.

This was only until she noticed the guy in the car next to hers..her dad!

It seemed like their Titanic has got its first iceberg hit.

Later that night came the icing on this shitty day! When she realized that in all the hodgepodge, she has forgotten to buy herself a pack of sanitary pads.

But the power of love saved her as she tried to look in her cupboard with a "maybe" and finds the kurta that Suraj gifted her, wrapped around "her precious"

BAAP-TISM

It'd been 10 days since Sneh's dad saw her with Suraj, He hadn't asked Sneh anything yet and was acting as if nothing has happened. Though inside Sneh knew what's going on inside him!

Sneh could not handle the tension between them anymore and decided to make the first move herself when her dad was about to leave for office

Sneh: Papa! I need to talk to you..

Dad still tried to avoid the situation and started rushing toward the door like he hasn't heard her

Sneh: PAPA!! (she shouts in anger..)

He stopped right there

Dad: What?

Sneh: You saw me with a guy last Sunday!

Dad: I don't know what you're talking about..*koi aur hoga!*

Sneh: No!..It was you.. I saw you clearly.

Dad: OK..haan!.. I saw you with your friend..so what? Must be just friend..what's the big deal?

Sneh: It is a big deal!..He is my boyfriend!.. more than a boyfriend in fac

Dad: No!..You're lying!

Sneh: Why would I lie? He is my boyfriend and i think we really have a future.

Dad: Good..must be a great guy, tell me when I should meet him? Though I really think you're smart enough to choose for yourself...

Sneh (interrupted him): PAPA WHAT IS WRONG WITH YOU!! You have seen me with this guy, who clearly does not have any quality that a father would look for, and I'm telling you that he's MORE THAN A BOYFRIEND to me and you're asking me when should you meet him?

Dad: WHAT AM I SUPPOSED TO DO THEN?..Scold you? HIT YOU? Tell me? You probably won't listen or understand any of what I'll say..make me a villain here and then this guy will take your side on all your impractical plans.. and eventually you will do whatever you want to.. so, what's the point?

You grew up so quick, i just have never pictured myself in this situation and I really don't know what to do or say here! It seems just like yesterday when i used to buy little dresses for you.

Sneh: It actually was yesterday when you got me a little dress..papa, but I have grown up, and I know you are right and Suraj may not seem perfect, but he is a nice guy.. you have to take a chance on relationships, right?.. And I want to take my chance with him.

Dad: Why don't you give me a chance first?.. I am your dad..don't I deserve a chance?

Sneh: You want me to see a guy, for like arranged marriage?

Dad: No, all I want is..see.. you guys have spent time together, so who always leads the way? Who decides what to do? Where to go? And more importantly..who pays the bills? You, right? I just want you to spend a day with this guy, but think of it as you're in the future, and let this guy lead and decide everything, let him pay from his per day income. I know you aspire to be an independent working woman, but just for a day.. see what all this guy has to offer.

Sneh: I don't know what you are trying here papa, but we have spent a lot of days and he decides some things too. If you are saying to just spend a day with him on his money..sure.. I'll do that tomorrow.

Dad: No, not tomorrow, it has to be a special day for this special occasion.. your birthday! It is just a few weeks ahead, just spend your this year's birthday with him and see how you will have all your days later. I am not even compelling you to do this, it's just a friendly request, hope that's the least you could do for your father..*nahi?*

Sneh (took a deep breath as she saw her dad all teary eyed): Whatever you say papa..and thanks for not getting ridiculously mad at me. At least I am not a lesbian..she felt like saying.

With only a minor move of our planet around the sun, the day was here even before Sneh would have cared to discuss her dad's request with Suraj or even know what his per day income was. But she did after her dad reminded her again a day before.

It was Rs 300.. 9000 divided by 30. When Sneh asked her dad, if there's any time duration he wanted her to be with him.

"from 7 in the morning till 7 in the evening maybe" he said without being too precise.

HAPPY? BIRTHDAY

After a subtle gong from the big wall clock at 5, the most disgusting sound, a beeping alarm from the table clock at 5:30, and 3 orchestral and vibrating snoozes on the mobile phone at 5:40, 5:50 and 6:00, she somehow opens her eyes as she has to leave home before seven.

6:00 am

The bed felt like quicksand, pulling her as much as she tried to get out of her silky bed sheet and cozy blanket. Her father on the other hand was busy absorbing his daily dose of news by reading the newspaper and simultaneously surfing between various news channels, whilst enjoying his morning cup of *chai*.

As she came wandering in to the room and stood like a zombie close to the sofa, her dad looked up confused and said: What?

She (hoping that he didn't forget her birthday): What?

Dad: Whaaaaat?

He couldn't hold it any more, and burst out laughing "Happy Birthday *mera bacchaa!!* I was just playing!" and hugged her.

"God bless you *beta*..and give you some brains as you are too pretty already!" he said

"Thank you very much papa and I hate you" she said referring to his idea about the day that she was dreading and speaks up in the same breath "Where's my gift?"

Dad: You were born around 8 in the evening, so you'll get that later only. (Cleverly buying time to think about something as he had failed to get her anything yet)

She dragged herself to the washroom vigorously rubbing her eyes, and widely yawning sat on the toilet pot and as her eyes started to adjust to the bright bathroom light, she saw there are no books on the little rack next to the seat.

She: Mummmay!! (she squeaked..) Where are my damn books?

(Her mom was still sleeping, but her dad was right outside the bathroom door)

Dad: *Beta* those are really expensive books! Do you think you want to spend that much so early in the day?

She: Whaaatt? Come on papa!.. You know I can't go without reading (she screamed, annoyed)

Dad: I know beta, but I don't give a shit about your shit today. You know, Suraj the Great takes care of you now, and there is today's Hindi newspaper there. And don't worry, that's free.

She: Yeah right! Like the first thing I want to read in the morning is about how many rapes and murders happened yesterday!

Even Before she had woken up to her senses completely, her day started to seem different already as she had never experienced any denial to her wants and needs ever. Turning on the geyser, she was shocked to see that the tiny red light didn't turn on.

She shouted again: Papa!! Did you do something to the geyser as well? It's not working!

Dad (laughing): No beta, it hasn't been working since last night.. You want me to call a guy to fix it?

Her dad was loving every moment of this day as he had always wanted to put some money value in her head, but loved her too much to say no to any big or small wants that she had.

By now Sneh had understood her dad's whole 'Make her day hell so she would break up with Suraj plan' and decided to take on the challenge with full fervor!

"NOPE dad!! It's not even cold today. We'll see tomorrow." she said, looking up dramatically at the shower head, grabbed the knob like she is about to pull a trigger on herself and her inner over dramatic voice goes "Anything for you Suraj..anything!!" and turned it on.

"Huahhhhahauhhahaahaaa... ohhhh fuuuuaaaackkkkkk..huuuh huhu hhu its damn colrrrdhhhhh" Sneh screamed from the bathroom.

But strangely, within 5 seconds she realized that she is not actually feeling too cold. So she smiled and opened the drawers hunting for her vanity essentials. But to her dismay, there is no fancy moisturizing soap, no fancy body wash, no loofah, no 'organic-double-the-normal-rate' shampoo, no tried by Bollywood heroine's damage control conditioner, but only a tiny bar of hamam soap.

She cursed her dad with an "arrrrrhh" and started rubbing the soap on her body, this boring cheap-ass bath took her only 8 minutes instead of her normally over 20 minutes. Getting ready without any makeup didn't take her much time either.

She shouted out: *"Chhotu breakfast laga de!"*

Suddenly her dad appeared out of nowhere, waiting for this opportunity to say: Do you know his per day salary? It must be equal to your guy's...so I don't think you guys can afford him!

She: Phew! Fine, I can manage. I can make my own breakfast! Do we have Meggi?

Dad: Yeah there is a box full of it.

She got into the kitchen asking where?

Dad: In that store, right across the street.

She was not impressed by any of her dad's tactics anymore and gave a little snort of laughter thinking how wrong her dad is in thinking that just one day could make any difference to her love for Suraj.

She hopped across the street and made the first purchase on her limited budget birthday.

Minus Rs. 20 Rs. 280 Left

She strictly followed the instructions on the packet, and gorged on the Meggi proudly (though it took way more than 2 minutes to cook), combed her hair which were rather unmanageable on that particular day, thanks to the absence of her pricey hair products, picked her bag, plugged in her iPod and started to walk out of the house to meet Suraj, when her dad's voice again pierced her heart saying: Do you want to use MY iPod for a day?

Now she got really pissed-off, gritting her teeth said "No, I don't want to use YOUR iPod or YOUR handbag or ANYTHING! I'll be just fine with my Rs. 300".

Dad (correcting her with a grin): 280! Now here you go, take this old not-so-smart phone and give me yours for the day.

aiyahhhh

She took it with a huff and stomped out.

She did not want to spend too much out of her limited budget, so she was pondering which bus to take when her mom's creepy 'soapy kurta spots' episode came to her mind and she shuddered and quickly boarded an auto, but very soon got off as the guy was not willing to go by the meter. The third guy she stopped agreed, even though inside she had no idea how to read or calculate fare from a meter.

On the way she suddenly spotted an open chemist shop, from where she had to buy her kind of asthma pump without which she cannot survive for more than an hour… a lip balm (though the cheapest one today with no flavor or colour)

Minus Rs. 10 Rs. 270 left

7:15 am

Sneh reached the meeting spot all dirty and wheezing and paid for the auto.

Minus Rs. 20 Rs. 250 left

Suraj was already there, excited as ever. He hurriedly hugged and lifted her half a feet up saying "Happy birthday!"

Sneh: Thank you very much. Where is my gift?

Suraj: Gift? *Gift ke paise kahan hain, aaj ki shart bhool gyi kya?*

She made a sad face, but then, Suraj took out a "necklace" from his back pocket. It's a super cheap somewhat imitation of Kate's necklace from the Titanic. Instead of the ocean, it was heart of the roadside Sunday bazaar, which he had got from his Sunday bazaar colleague for free, so no price deduction here!

She took it happily thinking that though she will never wear it, but it will still be a good idea to keep it as a weird memory of this weird birthday. She handed over the remaining budget money to Suraj as she did not either have a pocket or a bag.

7:30

They sat there in front of a small super bazaar as they planned for their day ahead. They looked around and saw that no shop has opened yet except for the dairy, where the guy is setting up his milk carts, and there is a chai wala buzzing with his loyal morning crowd, and there are some sleepy sloppy school kids at a bus stop waiting for their ride to the day ruining building.

They ordered two glasses of *chai* (low sugar for Sneh), two fans and started talking.

Minus Rs. 20 Rs. 230 Left

If we ever get married you will be the one to wake up early to get milk, turn on the motor for water and all, as I cannot wake up this early. And if we ever had babies…you would have to settle them when they cry at nights.. she said.

He agreed on the morning part but said "I can't promise handling all the kids, as I can only handle maximum three at once."

With this joke he thought of cheering her up but what got her to jump on to her feet was seeing a cyber café being opened.

Suraj: *Pagal hai kya? Net kyun use karna hai subah subah?*

Sneh: Arre kal maine apne birthday ki saari parties cancel kardi thi, tou jis jis ne mujhe abhi tak wish nahi kiya hoga, use apni friend list se delete kar dungi!

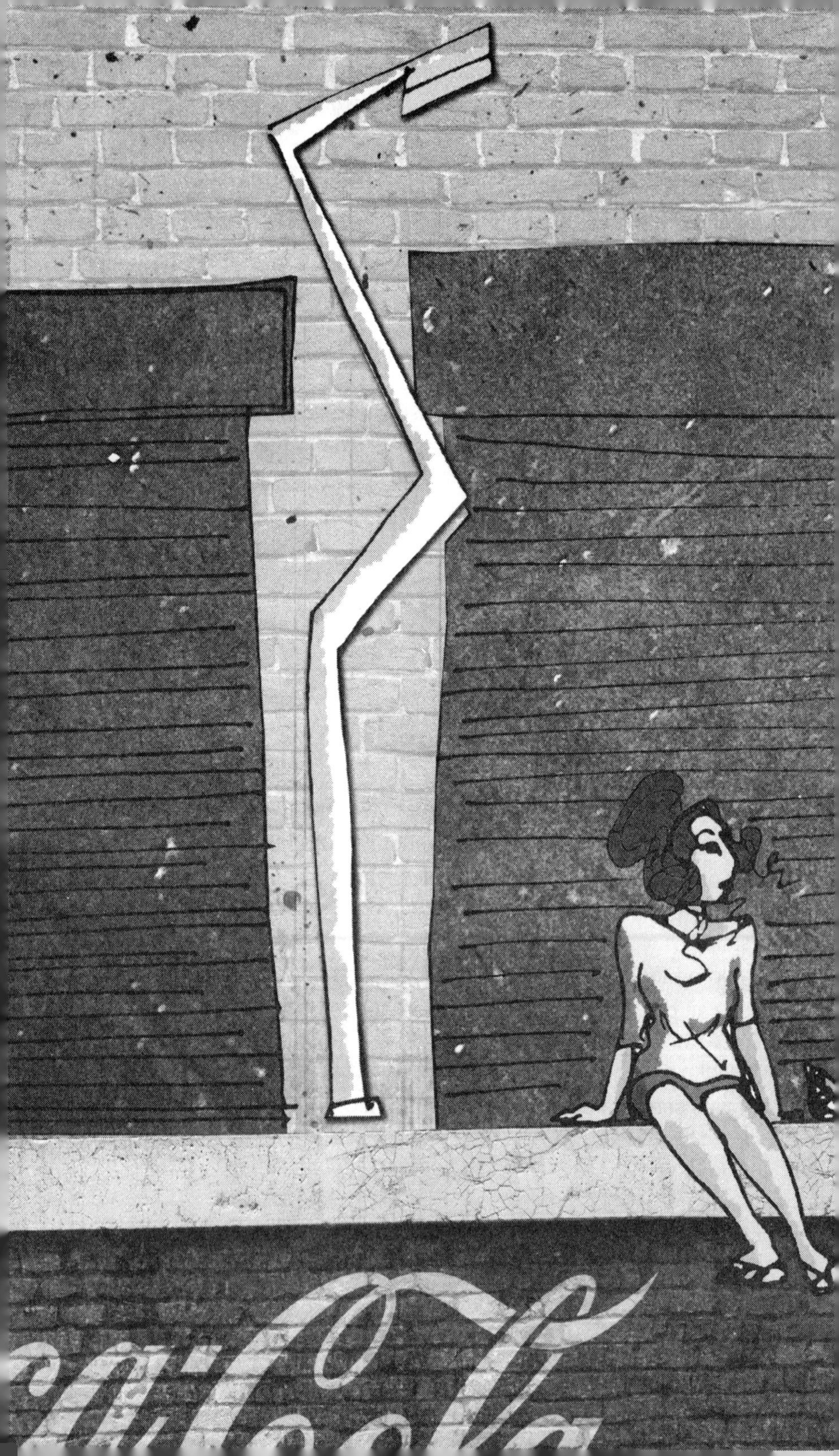

Suraj: *Tou kal karlena!*

She: *Na! Abhi karna hai, baad mein mujhe har wish ka time dekhna parega.*

Almost everyone had wished her, thanks to Mark Zuckerburg, because now people who would miss even their wife's and mother's birthdays, and had to face the outrage, now don't miss out their farthest of friends' and relatives' birthdays.

Minus Rs. 20 Rs. 210 left

After Sneh was satisfied with her social networking, they wondered where they can spend their time till the mall, movie theatres and restaurants open for business. Also, they did not have that kind of money. Only God could salvage them from this situation, and thus as Suraj suggested, they took a metro to Gurudwara Bangla Sahib.

Minus Rs. 30 Rs.180 Left

After getting out of the metro, Suraj asked the fair till Gurudwara from an auto guy.. *Pachchas*!! Came the heart breaking reply!

Suraj: *30 le lena bhaiya, 50 jyada bata rahe ho!*

Auto guy didn't even care to answer back..

Meanwhile Sneh saw a cycle renting stand there and joked *"Cycle le lein kya?" :p*

Suraj took it as an idea so good and even with Sneh refusing he got the cheapest one for Rs. 30 for one and a half hour.

Minus Rs. 30 Rs. 150 Left

8:30 am

Suraj seemed to be enjoying riding the cycle but for Sneh it was all "auu.. auu.. auu" sitting on the uncomfortable carrier and passing all Delhi road bumps!

Stop stop stop stop…she goes suddenly, as Suraj stopped the cycle with brakes supported by his hawaii chappals, and turned to see what had happened. She was already off the carrier and was squatting and playing with a tiny black and white puppy! Wait there is one more who is brown, wait, two more white ones, wouo..and a complete black one, it seemed like some university brochure with at least one student from every ethnicity.

Suraj (after 10 minutes): *Chal ab..kabhi puppy nahi dekhe kya? :p*

Sneh: *Nahi..ye wale kahan dekhe kabhi.*

Suraj: *Kyun, car mein kitni baar tou yahin se jati hai*

Sneh: *Car park karni padrti hain na :p teri khatara cycle ka kuch tou faeda ho!.. chup reh!*

"Ello chhotu puppy.. elo elo elo.. aja.. aja mumma pass"

Not so happy to hear, their real mumma came out of nowhere with a bad scary face..

Slowly, she got up and sat on the carrier that now seemed perfect to ride away.. *"bye chhotus.. bye mumma ji"* she said, relieved, waving at the little drowsy walking puppies while she herself was not too stable sitting backwards on the cycle carrier.

After 10 minutes of butt hurting adventure for Sneh and *"sardi mein bhi garmi ka ehsaas"* for Suraj, they reached their destination.

9:00 am

As soon as they entered the premises, they were welcomed by bright white walls, monochrome tiles and devotees of all shapes, sizes and ages queuing up to pay homage. As they entered the main building, there is a serene calm disturbed by a few toddlers running and performing some yet-to-be-named yoga asanas, on the comfortable no-injury wall to wall carpet. Slow tempo tabla beats with humming vocals calmed their tensed nerves, and made them feel like there is still some promise left in this hostile world… for them & for everyone.

They followed the crowd unaware of the customs, but with a little monkey see monkey do, they did just fine. Covering their heads and bowing to the revered Guru Granth Sahib, and for once donating Rs.10 without worrying about their meagre budget.

Minus Rs. 10 Rs. 140 left

Sneh may have kind of believed in God but was not that religious or even understood a single word from the prayer, but she felt like the prayer guy is telling her that she has taken the right path, it will all be alright and there shall be a lifelong of beauty, peace and love. Suraj on the other hand just felt like crying but somehow he managed to control himself. He felt completely vulnerable, and silly, fearing he was doing something wrong and that he is just not good enough for her.

They sat quietly in the hall, thinking about their future together. Suraj asked God to get them together only if it is good for her, only if she could live happily with him, as he began doubting his ability to meet her daily needs, let alone her fancy lifestyle in the long run.

They sat near the sparkling sarovar eating the delicious *'Karha parsad'*, and then with their pants raised above their ankles they started touching the plump grey and orange moustached fish swimming near the shore.

They felt so good to find that there are still things in this world which come without a price tag. After a good while they started taking a walk around the sarovar holding hands, but are very soon objected by an old lady whose shouting *"Oye, hath chhadd ke challo, eh garden nyi haiga!"* brought forth a titter.

Even though they only understood the word "garden", but deciphered the seriousness of their offence from her expressions, and quickly left hands.

Sneh was feeling bad and thought that maybe even God is against their love, but Suraj pacified her saying "No, it's just the people, not God!" as he pointed towards the Langar hall.

Langar is a delicious free meal served in the gurudwara with the concept of rich and poor to eat together. They were rich and poor together already but they could use a free meal on this day more than any other. Sneh and Suraj kept raising their hands (properly joined together as suggested by the person doing *sewa*) again and again for the *rotis*, till they were stuffed full, both physically as well as spiritually.

Sneh kept objecting in order to save money, but Suraj forced her to buy a *kadaa* (bangle) from one of the many shops lined outside the gurudwara.

Minus Rs. 20   Rs. 120 Left

9:50 am

Looking at the rented cycle, it came to their mind that it was theirs not forever but just one and half hour to which only 10 minutes were left. They could not afford a rip-off today where they might have to pay for another half an hour. They needed to get back fast and it seemed like a job for stronger legs…so yes, they took the right decision and let Sneh "Handle" it!

So she cycled fast, over taking the surprised traffic like a superwoman,

making them reach only a few minutes late for the return. Thankfully, good enough for not being overcharged!

10.05

After returning their cycle they took a walk to a nearby place Janpath.. which is an open market with people haggling for brand imitation apparel, sunglasses and bags which are highly affordable if you know the art of negotiation. Unfortunately, on that day, even Janpath was out of their reach considering their current balance of Rs.120. But just out of habit, Sneh started browsing through some tops with a very keen interest of buying. One of the tops caught her eye and she asked the price. She was expecting anything between Rs. 600-1000, thanks to her brand conscious sensibilities, but was astonished at the shopkeeper's reply of Rs.350. But then suddenly her face became pale thinking that she cannot even afford it at this price. However, she still tried to keep her ego putting blame on the shop guy *"Bhaiya patla sa tou hai material, 100 ka de do" she said* and moved on...Sneh had just taken a step when suddenly he, with the top already packed in a polythene bag called her: *"le lo madam".*

Sneh (looking for an excuse): *Abhi rakho bhaiya, cash nikaal ke aate hain.*

Bhaiya: *Ye raha madam* (pointing towards the ATM machine right behind his shop).

Sneh could have said anything to him, or could have just walked away as she was not answerable to him but for some unknown reason, she felt like coming clean.

Sneh: *Bhaiya yaar..aaj paise nahi hain.. ATM sheyTM kahin bhi nahi... 300 rupaye leke ghar se nikale the, pata bhi nahi chala aur 200 kharch hogaye!.. Ab 100 ke aas pass hi bache hein, jisme sham ko kuch khayenge.. fir ghar wapis bhi jana hai.. lumbi kahani hai.. aap polythene mein hi rakhna bus, main next time aake jaruur lungi, kisi ko dena mat please.*

Bhaiya (his heart melted like an ice cream on a hot summer day hearing of her fashion-crisis): *Ye lo, le jao aap. Paise de jana jab bhi ho.*

She was amazed by this sudden kindness and went *"Haan?..Sach mein?* Bhaiya you are the greatest..*bas aapki wajeh se hee ye desh abhi tak chal raha hai. Warna kab ka duub gya tha!"*

The shopkeeper just smiled shyly in return as they walked out of the market as she was all laughters and overwhelmed.

11:00

They started to roam around the Rajiv Chowk inner circle, as they walked past various big brand's showrooms, the gatekeepers pulled the gate open, invitingly. Considering the amount they had left in the pocket, after a while this lively marketplace which was Sneh's second favourite after the malls, started to feel embarrassing and suffocating.

"Chal aaj tujhe jannat ki seyr karata hun" Suraj exclaimed.

"Jannat?" She was puzzled, yet uninterested.

"Haan..purani Dilli.. matlub Old Delhi' Suraj proclaimed.

'Eww..purani Dilli :p Jamna-Paar na chale jayein" The sarcasm in her tone was pretty apparent.

'Chal ke dekh tou sahi ek baar..teri weeran South Dilli se tou acha hi hai!" Suraj retaliated.

After a bit of argument, silence fell over them, as the door of the Soni showroom opened, and made way to the cheering of kids playing cricket on the latest gaming consoles with their spectacled eyes glued to monstrous LED screens.

She realized that they don't have much of options. So, half-heartedly or maybe with no heart at all, they were walking down Minto Bridge which divides the city into two parts, Old and New. When you cross this bridge, which is hardly one and a half kilometer long, it feels like you have time traveled back to the Mughal era.

Although it was just a kilometer, all this walking made her exhausted and she was sweating like a pig.

"Aur kitna chalaega? I am dying hungry" She cribbed, as a ball hit her forehead.

"Welcome to purani Dilli" Suraj declared jubilantly.

Bunch of fluttery kids ran towards them to get their ball back, she was amazed to see that there are still places where kids play cricket outside of gaming consoles. She threw the ball over to them.

"Shukriya didi" they all shouted, thanking her, somehow it sounded like a warm welcome to her.

12:00

"Bata..kya khaegi?" Suraj asked pointing toward tiny labyrinth lanes and bylanes almost choked with bunks and carts, loaded with hot and fiery food. The highly inviting aroma tantalized their nostrils, as Suraj struggled against the swarming ravenous people to get his favourite *Haleem*.

Meanwhile, Sneh was spellbound looking at the kebab seller, who skillfully took a meatball, spread it evenly over a *"seekh"*, and put a thread around in such a way that when he pulls it after grilling, the kebab is finely cut into five exquisite pieces.

Impressed with this magical performance Sneh wanted to try that first, so Suraj had to take this Mission Impossible 2.

Minus Rs 40 Rs 80 Left

With their stomachs more than full they again started to wander in the lanes of Chandni Chowk. As they walked past Jama Masjid, a woman squatting with mysterious herbs and shrubs called Suraj to come closer.

"Oye nakli hero! YE KYA HAAL BANA RAKHA HAI! suukh ke tila hora hai.. ye le Totka-e-Mardana, MARD BAN MARD.. aur le Neel Nitin Mukes podder lgaa, madam jesa chikna banja, ye Bengali Surma! Madam ki aankh mein daal de, teri mohabbat mein aisa padregi ke kisi aur ki taraf dekhegi bhi nahi!" She stops after elaborating the baffling prescription.

"Sab kuch mila ke kitne ka padrega?" Suraj seemed totally intrigued when Sneh literally dragged him away clutching his wrist.

After a while, Sneh's stomach started to feel funny but she choose not to tell Suraj about it, as she didn't want to come up as a high society softy who couldn't even handle one roadside snack. She also got nauseous and dizzy. Before she totally lost her balance, sat on a footpath with a thump and asked Suraj to get a bottle of water.

Minus Rs10 Rs 70 Left

"Theek tou hai?" Suraj asked.

"Haan haan" She said and took a few gulps and splashed her face.

She got her composure back, and got up, brushing the dirt off her shorts, her eyes fell on a small A4 sized poster on the wall. She smiled and nudged Suraj to take a look. It's a B or maybe C grade horror movie poster titled *"Hasina Bani Dracula"*, featuring a lady in her mid 30's as Dracula with blood dripping from her long fangs but not longer than her revealing cleavage! There is also a horse with his forelegs up, a few guys with old school guns and a teenage boy, who is yet to get his first facial hair, probably the hero, making it clear that this movie would be anything but boring.

Smiling at it they both made their way ahead, the same poster was visible at every 10 feet, and every time it caught their eyes they saw something new in it. 2 minutes on the same path, there was a bigger version of the same poster and this time it's not on a wall. It's on a dirty cloth, probably an old filthy bed sheet from the last century or maybe a sari of lady who invented and first wore it. It was a tattered mess with only 5% colour saturation. As they were busy staring at it, they notice that something is flickering in the background.

Suraj did have an idea of what to expect, but he still opened the cloth to confirm. As expected, there is this really old television set and a redundant VCR being stared at by some 20 odd people, like a *"firang"* roaming the streets of Tilak Nagar. They looked like labor class people watching the climax scene of *"Hasina bani Dracula"* with immense interest as if it was based on their own true story.

Suraj hastily put the curtain back as the audience seemed to be distracted. Sneh stood there like a deer in headlights, hardly blinking her wide eyes.

Suraj jokes: *Dekhni hai kya?*

Sneh spits out her answer in a jiffy: *"Aur kya!"*

There is an old guy, as tattered as the curtain, smoking beedi and holding used bus tickets in his stubby hand. These are actually the make believe tickets of the exciting show going on inside. Sneh had never seen anything like this before! Her excitement reached one notch higher, when she noticed that the tickets are priced at Rs.10 each!

Minus Rs. 20 Rs. 50 Left

Contrary to their expectations, nobody emerged from behind the cloth for over 20 minutes. They assumed that either the audience is in for a back to back viewing of the awesome movie, or they are the staff people having

हसीना बनी
DRACULA

their *gutkha* infested incomprehensible chatting, baring brick coloured tainted teeth, which can give the *Hasina* Dracula a run for her money.

So they stepped inside, find a comparatively cleaner spot to sit, eagerly waiting for the movie to start, so that the other audience members would stop staring at her.

1:00 pm

Dhen Dhennn Dheinnnn!!

The movie started with banging loud orchestral music that can bring all your senses to immediate attention. People started looking at the TV now, but whenever a scene with the heroine would appear, at least two of the guys would look back at her, grinning shamelessly.

Along with the deepening of the film plot, the heroine's cleavage also got deeper and deeper. This led Sneh into a reflex of pulling the back hem of her kurta downwards after every 5 minutes.

The plot of the movie, like every other Bollywood movie was quite predictable, with the heroine's dad getting run over by a speeding jeep full of drunk, armored, loud laughing, trigger happy, potential womanizers having a fun night of debauchery. As he struggles for life in a dim-lit hospital, her poor daughter goes door to door in need of blood that is required to save her dad's life. Most of the poor and selfish village people clearly said "no" on her face, which seems quite genuine considering their waif like anemic bodies, more in need of blood for themselves!

Thokar after thokar, the overly optimistic girl approaches the same bunch of gangster dudes who ran over her dad. They all look healthy and young, will definitely help, she thought, However, what she missed out was that these healthy young lads had more hormones in their bodies than blood.

So going by the age old C grade Bollywood movie formula, they, ad nauseam, rape her, strangle her and hang her from a tree branch. So, after much thunder and lightning, she comes back from the dead to get the one simple thing she couldn't get while being alive.. Blood! The only difference being, that earlier she needed B+, but now any blood group will do!

The whole idea of the movie was skin show, so much so that there should have been a tag line under the film title.. "*Hasina Bani Dracula*..a cleavage in 90% of the shots."

As the "interval" text flashed on the not so big screen, Sneh felt an urge to eat something and to use the bathroom. But there is none available. She asked Suraj if he could ask someone about the bathroom. Suraj immediately responded *"Haan hai na!"* He then took her outside and after walking a few steps pointed upwards to a huge yellow hoarding and proudly said "M for *Mutralay!*".

While she used the MkDonald's washroom, he bought popcorn for Rs.10 from a roadside vendor, the quantity in the newspaper bag was equal to the Rs.300 tub you get at a multiplex, but yeah, they put like a whole pack of salt in that tub too :p. The popcorn added to all the cheap thrill they got from the hard core C grade gore fest having blood which is more orange than red.

Minus Rs. 10 Rs. 40 Left

The guy sitting next to Suraj was constantly throwing irritated looks at him, annoyed by his popcorn crunching noise, to which Suraj offered him some from his packet. But he refused, and now smiling, offered him a puff from the *beedi* he was holding between his purple scaly lips. Suraj took the beedi from his hand and took a puff. He then took a new one from the guy and offered it to Sneh, but she refused saying "*Beedi? Aye haye..tu ye bhi peeta hai?"*

Suraj: *Nahi aisa nahi hai! Waise hee.. Kabhi kabhi.. Wese tum bhi tou apni uss friend ke saath share kar rahi thi, jisko flat dilwaya tha!*

Sneh: *Abe wo cigarette thi!!*

Suraj: *Tou? Usse kark rog nahi hota kya?*

Sneh: (making a weird face, thanks to his weird hindi usage.. snatches the beedi from his fingers, takes a long puff and says) *Bas ye last hai tumhari ..haan!*

Suraj (with a smile): *Haan.. Hameshan last hee hoti hai!*

However, they continued smoking from the packet of the friendly smoker till their heads started feeling funny & now the movie seemed to appear in high definition format.

Suraj started repeating the dialogues and she started laughing for no reason. Yes, those were not your regular *beedis*, they had some weed mixed in them. Sneh started feeling like her smile is stretching beyond her face and that she has wriggly snakes for hair.

Suraj, highly inspired by Titanic, felt like they are on a boat in the rugged sea with all these pirates for company, and there is a storm coming and they all will probably die.

After 45 minutes Suraj woke up and noticed there were new and few faces in the tent and that the movie had started again. He woke Sneh up, who was drooling on his shoulder and helped her out.

He checked his pocket to realize the most predictable cliché.. Their money was gone!

Minus Rs. 40 Rs. 0 Left

Suraj thought about not telling her and tried to figure out something, but he knew they have to take a rickshaw right then to the metro station as she was in no condition to walk that long a distance.

She had already hailed a rickshaw while Suraj was still wondering what to say.

Sneh: What happened?

Suraj: *Wo… Paise nahi hain!*

She: *Paise nahi hain?.. Kyun hai tou 40 rupaye..baad ki baad mein dekhenge.. abi tou chal ghar ke paas.*

Suraj: *Nahi yaar, kuch bhi paise nahi hain, kisi ne chura liye movie mein!*

Sneh: (got down from the rickshaw): *Kya keh raha hai yaar..dubara check kar honge.*

Suraj: (checks his pocket again): *Nahi hain.*

Sneh: *Ab ghar kya chal ke jaenge itni duur?? AUR PHUNKO BEEDIYAN APNE BIHARIYON KE SATH!!.... phewwwww…*

Suraj: *MOVIE TOU TUJHE HI DEKHNE KA JOSH CHADRA THA! Aur main Bihari nahi hun, UP ka hun.*

Sneh: *Haan UP tou badra UK hai na!.. Papa sahi keh rahe the!*

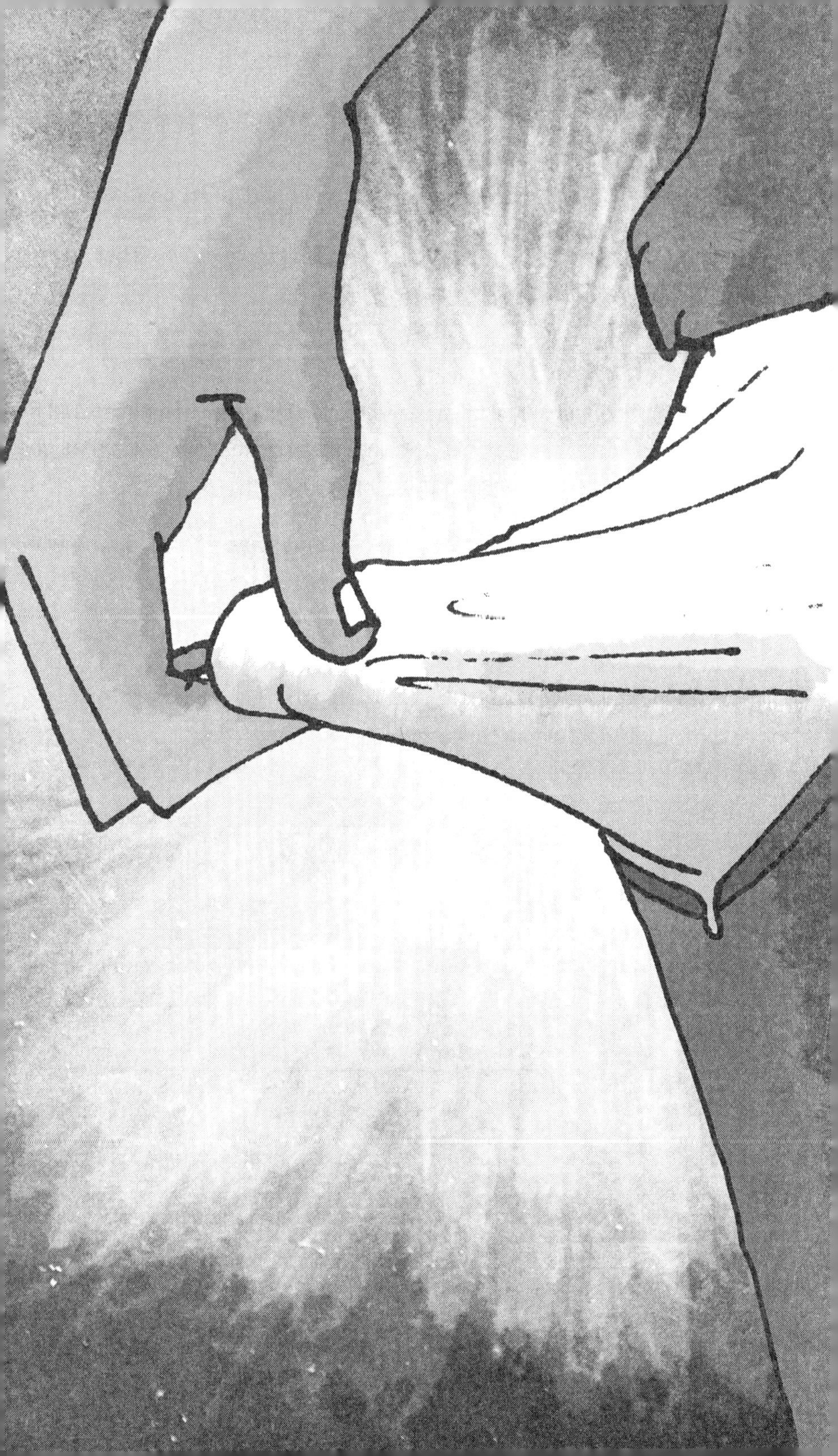

Suraj: *Haan tou phir nahi aana tha.. Papa ki godi mein hee rehna tha.. unke bina wese bhi tu kuch nahi kar sakti.*

Sneh: *Tere se tou jyada hi kar sakti hun..*

Suraj: *Haan tou phir kar le naa phir..KALAP KYUN RAHI HAI!*

"Haan..kar lungi jab karna hoga.. maine tou socha tha maine Bihar.. nyi.. UP ka maharaja fasaa liya hai, ab bus aish karungi beth ke but.." She said with a smile and landed a soft punch on his shoulder.

As the tension between them eased down, their focus shifted to the bigger problem at hand.

4:00 pm

With no money at all, even the overcrowded, bustling old Delhi felt like a desert. All the food, water, conveyance etc are unavailable, it's unbelievable how the environment changes when you have no money at all..it's like you are stranded on an uninhabited island.

They now had no reason to walk, or to look for anything, they couldn't even think of what to talk about.

They could have taken an auto home and paid him there, but that would mean they failed...failed to live even a single day on the expected scenario of their future.

She broke the awkward silence with a more awkward statement

"Bhookh lag rahi hai yaar..tu kahin se bread nahi chura sakta kya?"

Suraj was knocked out of his thoughts as he looked up and smiled, wondering how quickly the circumstances can bring someone from high society to the thoughts of stealing.

stranded in the city

Just as they were wondering what to do, a cart guy loaded with boxes asked them to move aside and make way.

Suraj's eyes lit up & he says: *Hum aur paisa kamaa sakte hain... hai na?*

Sneh: *Matlub?*

Suraj: *Apne papa se puch ki hum aur paisa kamaa sakte hain aaj ke liye?*

Sneh: OK.

Calls her dad.

Sneh: *Papa hum aaj ke din mein hee aur paisa kamaa sakte hain na?*

Dad (trying to control his smile): Yes *beta*, you can earn as much as you want and if you make too much money, please book a Range Rover for me..black!

Sneh: Yeah right! *Noida mein flat lene ke baad bache tou jaruur karwa dungi :p* OK bye!

She disconnected the phone before her father could have even asked how it was going so far.

She: *Haan, kamaa sakte hain!*

Suraj ran to the guy with the cart and stopped him asking where he is coming from. He pointed to the direction of a wholesale shop. Suraj joined him on his round back and asked Sneh to wait at the *Mutralay*..err.. MkDonalds.

As she was standing there, a severe gastric discomfort forced her to rush to the washroom in MkDonald's. As she sat there in the washroom, she realized that "a happy release is happier than any happy meal".

As she decided to wait for Suraj in the restaurant, an old looking Japanese woman approached her, admiring the antique looking necklace that Sneh was wearing, she asked her where she had bought it from. Sneh recalled having seen an antique jewelry shop nearby and tried to give her the directions but the old lady couldn't follow her at all, so she decided to take her to the shop.

"It will still be better than killing time in a restaurant" She told herself. As they reached the shop, the old woman said to the shopkeeper- *"Nekkuresu..ordu nekkuresu"* in her Japanese accent. The shopkeeper looked perplexed, and helplessly looked at Sneh, as if asking her to translate. "She wants an antique necklace" She said, pointing towards her own.

As the shopkeeper displayed various ones, the old lady asked Sneh to pick the one that she likes the best. Not only that Sneh helped her choose, she also bargained the price, and took it to even lower than the half of original.

"Arigatou arigatou" the old lady showered her gratitude, as she pressed a Rs.500 note into Sneh's hand. She resisted at first, but then realised that given her current situation, she could have asked for a bigger note.

Meanwhile, Suraj had taken 5 rounds, shifting carts from a warehouse to a retail shop expecting Rs.100, as the owner had promised Rs. 20/round. However, he changed his statement and gave him only Rs. 50, saying that he had promised Rs.10/round.

Suraj took the money with a sullen face fearing he might have to lose the entire amount if he argues too much. He wanted to treat Sneh to her favourite meal at MkDonalds, and then drop her home in an auto, but now it did not seem possible with this meager amount.

Getting ripped off like that filled him with rage and he kind of hoped that one day, he would rip all these city people! And build a multiplex in his village.

mard Taange wala
main hun mard
maarega
mujhe
mujhe

Sneh called him on his phone, he asked her to wait for some more time.

With only Rs. 50 in his pocket, he went straight back to MkDonalds,despaired as if he had been robbed off his *"jaayedad"*.

Sneh rushed towards him and gave him a warm hug, showing him the crumbled Rs.500 note, as if it is the biggest amount they have ever seen.

*Plus Rs.550, But It all got controversial with this big amount being added to the day's budget, especially the 500 note which Sneh got just like that.

6:45 pm

Having had enough action for a day, they decided to return home now. Since it was not even 7 pm yet, instead of taking a rickshaw, they decided to walk down to the nearest metro station, Chandni Chowk. Sneh started to feel suffocated and nauseated again, partly because of the smoke filled narrow lanes, and partly owing to her upset stomach.

She wanted to tell Suraj about it, but her lungs were filled with air. Before she could have uttered a word, she threw up, trying to get a hold of Suraj's arm. He quickly held her and thumped her back, she coughed with tear-filled eyes, and the fits of vomit continued.

Suraj rushed to an auto, shouting "Stephens" and pushed Sneh inside. The auto zipped through the hoards of carts, rickshaws, and a never ending sea of people, and finally stopped outside the hospital.

It took the Doctor around 35 seconds to advise Sneh about staying hydrated and calling a nurse to give her a Katrolac injection. Later at the cash counter when they were asked to pay Rs.470, Suraj couldn't help feeling dizzy and nauseated while they walked towards the metro station.

Sneh was still feeling a bit weak, so they decided to board a lesser crowded train, the Delhi Metro being over crowded in the evening rush hour. They skipped 2 trains and boarded the third one, which was comparatively empty, but there was no chance to get a seat, thanks to the over enthusiastic people on the platform who run to grab seats, like being chased by zombies!

As soon as the doors were about to close with the oh so familiar 'ding dong ding dong' sound, a guy squeezed right though the gap, with a victorious look on his strangely designed bearded face with a twinkling ear stud. He walked past Suraj and Sneh, intentionally brushing the back of his hand on her behind. Sneh jumped forward in shock and gave him a dirty stare, all the more unable to understand what satisfaction such acts give these kind of people. Suraj stared at him too, but he was unabashed by his deed, and continued to stare with a suppressed grin.

To take their minds off the incident Sneh started asking about how much money is left. They counted the amount left, Rs.80 now, and found it sufficient for an auto ride home.

As soon as they heard the announcement for their station '*Agla station.....*' they started moving towards the door ready to push through and duck under stinking armpits. But Sneh suddenly noticed that Suraj has started moving in the opposite direction going for the door that is far. To her surprise, Suraj is initiating a handshake with that guy who molested her a while ago. As soon as their hands are gripped, Suraj pulls him and gives him a strong jerk forward, and BANG! headbutts him on the nose. By the time Sneh realised, she heard a sound like coming from the breaking of a thin wood plank. The lech had broken his nose making a trail of blood dripping on the floor. A few guys held Suraj back from further damage, while the injured guy sat on the floor with his hand cupping his nose. The speaker for coordinating with the train driver was used to stop the train, and all three of them were removed at the next station by the metro staff and taken to the control room.

They were not prepared for the next visual, that of the same policeman who had caught them a few months back in their car in the dim-lit alley. He came in, idly picking his teeth with a toothpick, and stopped with a jerk smiling wide, saying *"Oh ho... Sallu Bhai!! Aaj tou kapde puure pehne hue hain! Aaj konsa kaarnama kar rahe the bhai metro mein? Car bech di kya?"*

Sneh noticed 'Papa calling' flashing on her phone screen but put it on silent mode, and tried to reason with the policeman, explaining the sequence of events, but noted that there is a just a very placid smile on his face. She had noted elsewhere as well, that whenever someone met both of them together after some time, they smiled encouragingly, as if appreciating their love and commitment. Without further adieu, the policeman said *"Chalo iske first-aid ke paise do aur jao"*. Suraj asks how much, and is asked to give Rs.50.

As they handed over the money and started to walk away, the policeman calls from behind.. *"RECHARGE KRAA DENA!"*

9:15

After a lot of haggling for an auto ride, which normally would cost Rs.40, and moving for a kilometer on foot, she finally found an auto rickshaw willing to take her for Rs.30. They gave each other a warm but tired hug, like battered but victorious soldiers returning from a long war. Suraj walked back home, tired from the day's ordeal.

Just 5 minutes on the way, and the auto took a turn that she was not familiar with.

Sneh: *Bhaiya ye kahan ja re ho? Sidha jana tha!*

Auto driver (In a nonchalant tone): *Ye rasta chhota hai madam, bus 10 minute lagenge.*

Looking at his small body, age and strength she thought of him as a

harmless guy, yet tried to keep a track of where she is. She soon noticed the roads becoming less crowded and she began to worry. She looked at her mobile, the time is 9:45 pm.

Meanwhile Suraj had reached home.

As the traffic light turned green, two strange looking guys rushed towards the auto calling out the driver's name. They tried to sit in the auto, Sneh was about to protest, when another one materializes out of nowhere and sat next to her.

Sneh says loudly: *KYA KAR RAHE HO BHAIYA? UTRO NICHE!*

Driver (already had the three guys seated, two in the front and one with Sneh at the back, and had the auto running): *Bas ye aage tak jaenge madam, abhi utar jaenge.*

For once she thought about jumping from the other side, but could not muster the courage due to the speedy auto and rugged road.

Now she was panicked, her head got dizzy, vision had black flashes, and she started to sweat. She felt helpless, and all the scary news stories of rapes and harassment, that our city is so infamous for, churned in her head. How wrongly she had always blamed the victims for not being cautious themselves.. she thought.

She could not even call out for help, as the roads were empty, and the few cars passing by were at high speed. There was also no police vehicle in sight.

Trying to gauge the situation, she noticed that the 4 guys are now talking in some other language and laughing. She was sure they are talking about her from the few words she understood like *"Ameer"*, "Boyfriend" etc.

Her hands and knees were trembling with fear, and tears stung her eyes.

She hid her right hand below her knee and typed a message to Suraj, *"Auto wale ne 3 aur log bitha liye hain. Mujhe bohot darr lag raha hai."*

There was a faint message sent beep, which nobody was able to hear, but she still turned it to silent mode. Meanwhile, the guys continued looking back at her, pretending to be talking to the guy sitting next to her

Suraj was washing his face when he received her message, and luckily heard the beep in time, as he was waiting for her to call after reaching home. He came out of the bathroom rubbing his face with his shirt, picked up the phone and read the message.

His heart skipped a beat. He called her straight away, but heard a 'no balance remaining' message.

Sneh eagerly awaited a response from him, but got nothing. Now her tears had started to flow, slipping from her cheeks, dropping on her pants.

He tried messaging her *"Kahan hai auto"*, but it was not delivered, due to insufficient phone balance.

The auto took a sharp turn in a slum dwelling, she noticed a blue board overhead with half the description of a colony, and she immediately messages her Dad and Suraj 'Parm…Colony, in trouble'.

Suraj immediately understood the name and ran to his neighbor to borrow his bike. He called out his name but his mother came out in her garish nightgown: *Beta wo tou ghar nahi hai.*

Suraj: *Aunty bike bahar khadi hai. Mujhe bohut jaruri chahiye, chabi dedo please.*

Aunty went in, and came back with an excuse: *Beta chabi nahi mil rahi, wo saath hee le jata hai*

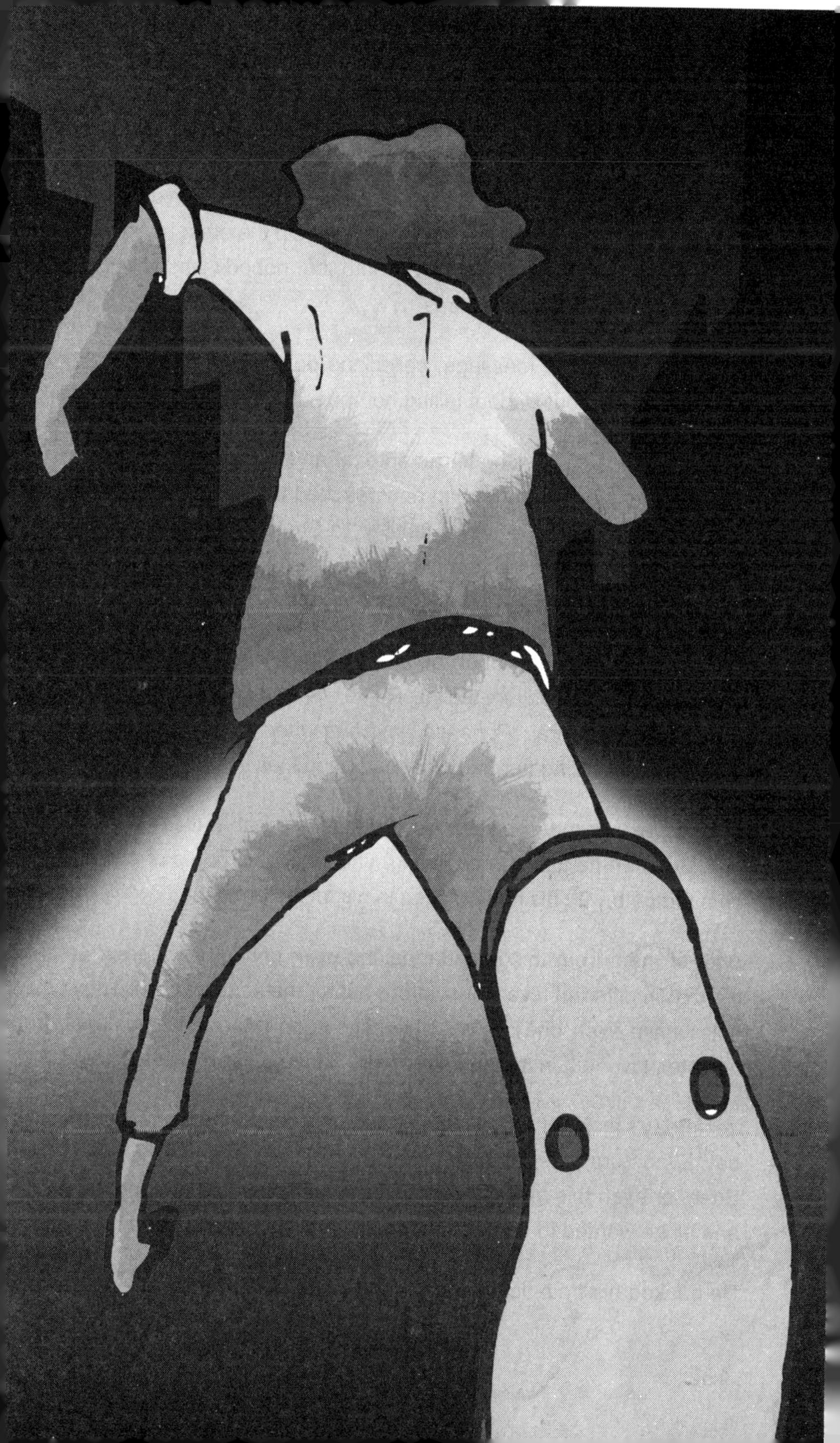

Meanwhile, the auto meanders its way deeper into the slum dwellings, and as the darker it got, the faster her heart beat. On the other hand Suraj was running on the roads looking for an auto, but nobody was willing to take him, in spite of his begging pleas.

Sneh's dad saw her message, called the police, and picked up his car keys and rushed out without telling her mom anything.

Suraj kept running, looking for an auto, or anyone who could give him lift. On the other side, the auto had now reached the end of the slum cluster to a wide road which seemed familiar to Sneh. The three guys got off, and the driver got back on the main road and within a minute she saw her colony lane and her dad about to get to his car.

The auto stopped, and Sneh gets off, finally breathing, wiping her eyes with her palm, handed him the last Rs.30 she had. Walking into her house, she messaged Suraj *"Pohonch gayi hun ghar"*, and rushed inside her house without telling her dad what had happened.

As soon as her message arrived, Suraj jumped at it, relieved to see the text. But then he just started crying, uncontrollable bouts of crying sitting on a footpath with his head hidden in his folded arms.

Both of them from this unusual pairing were crying, in different parts of the city, in different levels of comfort, but for the same reason. They could not survive even one day together. They had their good moments, fun, laughter, love, but in the end, they were a failure, their love was a failure.

Yesterday's incident shook her so badly, that Sneh had high fever the next day. Even Suraj was exhausted from all the stress, and had no guts to face Sneh, or even this messed-up city. He was having a throbbing headache and all he wanted to do was to go back to his hometown, and his mother.

He booked his train ticket and called Sneh to inform that he was leaving

and returning to his village forever. She tried consoling him saying that it was not his fault about the auto or the phone incident, but he was in no mood to listen.

Then she requested him to meet her for one last time before going to his hometown. At least to give her a chance to say goodbye, as they did not know when or if they would ever meet again. He replied a meek *'theek hai'* and also told her that he would return all her gifts.

They met at Kafé Coffee Day for this last time. There was this strange silence, this vacuum between them, that did not need words to convey their feelings, their angst, and the pain they were holding inside. He simply put the bag containing stuff gifted by her on the table.

She ordered her regular americano and very knowingly, his ice-laden frappachino.

He hardly looked at her, and kept playing with the religious thread around his wrist. She constantly stared at him with wet eyes, trying to decipher what is going on in his head, even though she herself was not sure about her own feelings.

Why are they not even talking!

Why is there no eye contact?

Why is there no sharing of drinks?

Why is everything far from the ordinary?

Before they knew it, they had finished their drinks, Sneh had paid the bill, and they started moving out of the outlet.

Just as they turned to go in their different directions, Sneh stopped and called out: *OYE SUNN!!*

Suraj stopped and turned towards her.

Sneh: *Ek baar aur try karien?*

Suraj goes into a deep thought, forgetting to even blink, and after a long pause says:

"Yeah.. why the fuck not?" (In an accent which was almost similar to her's)

Sneh laughed out, her eyes were still wet, and went near him clasping his hand into hers, ready for the challenges that await them. Suraj took the heavy bag with gifts from her shoulder and hanged it onto his, as they moved ahead planning their next date under only 200 with the idea of saving the remaining 100 for their future.. :)

EPILOGUE (from Sneh)

Sneh: It was that day and then all our days are kind of the same..

I and Suraj got married after 2 years, we did not need to elope or anything, I was never going to elope. I neither had the courage nor the conviction to do something so horrible to my parents. It was a love marriage in the pretence of an arranged one. There were a few guys who came to see me a couple of times, thanks to the over optimistic arrangements made by my mother. But none of it materialized because they kind of saw it on my face that I was having an affair. Or maybe on my arms and neck, thanks to the love bites I forced Suraj to give me a day before those guys were scheduled to come ;)

Our relation just kept going, getting stronger, and later, everyone just got bored of opposing us!

Now we are 5 years into our marriage, and have a kid "Leo", I am a freelance Costume Designer plus Homemaker, and Suraj is now a Realtor (better word for property dealer i guess).

Things are not dream-like. Almost every day starts like a game, everything brings with it, its share of struggle, a little bit of success, some hot some cold fights, mostly ending with laughter and a three-way hug with our little one. Almost every day we face some crisis, but we have learnt to plan, to strategize, to make ends meet to the best of our capabilities. And every night we sleep like a happy and content family.

"Pyaar se peyt nahi bharta" as sad as it may sound, is true. If I were an 80 year old famishing lady, locked up in a cage with no hope of getting out and being able to earn myself a living, I would definitely choose to extend my arm out from the cage and grab a packet of bread instead of a cuddly little pink teddy bear holding a heart, which on pressing produces a "puuuchhhhhhh" kissing sound, followed by 'I love you'. But I am not 80 years old, I am not famishing, and I don't think I owe anyone for my own extravagant dreams or even my *"do waqt ki roti"*. So get your packet of bread out of my sight! I would have that little teddy, which I would receive from someone with love. And if you really love someone with all your heart, you don't even have a choice!

Like we didn't have a choice! What we had was something directionless, pure, natural, young, stupid, impulsive and filmy, growing like a weed at its own will, without any knowledge of its own growth.

We were too entangled into each other, by the time we thought about breaking up. We could have returned each other's things & moved on, but we couldn't return the impact they have made on our lives. The feelings that are attached to them, the place that they have in our lives.

I could have returned all the good & bad quality downloaded movies he gave me, but not the laughs we had watching them. He could have returned all the Niike T-shirts and shoes back… but that would stink, literally!

I could definitely not return him that pack of whisper!

We couldn't return the rains to the clouds that fell on us and made us do.. well.. stuff.

I could return the 'heart of the ocean' from Sunday bazaar, but could not return his heart from my ocean..whaaaat??

In fact I had lost that heart piece right after our marriage, but found it a few days back while cleaning, so guess what he is going to get on his birthday in a few days? It may sound stupid to you but to him it will be his dream coming true. I'll let him draw me, wearing.."only" that! ;)

I guess we were and are soul mates..

He pays the rent

I pay the bills

I cook

He cuts the vegetables and salad

I still dream to be a hip housewife

He still struggles with English

He is still skinny and can't rape me

We fart and let fart

We have back aches

We have dreams and hope to make it big someday

We curse people with BMWs and Audis

We drink, we dance

We laugh, we fight, we cry, we smile

We are all right

And there is

Beauty.. Love..& Peace

Pyaar se peyt nahi bharta..true that! But that damn peyt is not the only organ in our body. There are other organs with equally important functions if not more, there is the heart, the brain, eyes, ears, skin..and some obvious organs that shouldn't necessarily be mentioned. All of these and our souls..can be filled with love..

and love only.

So this here was the story of Suraj and Sneh..

The last thing I would like to add is.. I really doubt if Suraj got to Sneh's house for the first time asking for address..“by chance”.

When I accused him that I think you somehow stalked Sneh and found her house..all he said was

“Aap jo marji samajh lo”..

Nishtha Chatterjee

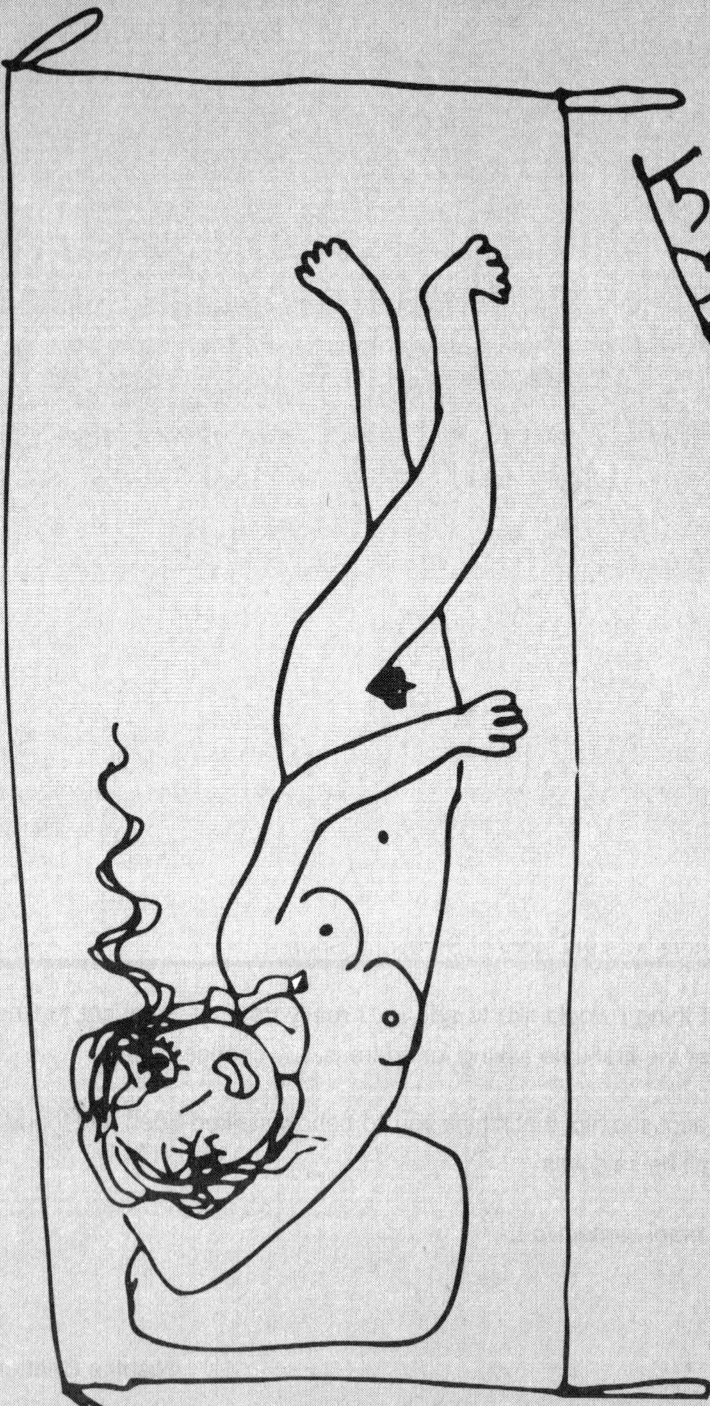

Acknowledgement

I would like to extend my gratitude to the main contributors of this book, Meisnam Jackson, our illustrator, Marshall the IIIrd, my husband's ridiculous sounding altar 'rapper' ego, and Danish Blessedone, our managing editor, who have been a very important part of my story. This book would not have been possible without the interesting illustrations of Meisnam Jackson, the grammar Nazism of Danish & the creative juices of Marshall the IIIrd which flow in all directions, required or otherwise.

I would also like to thank my friends and family for all their support and their being uncanny inspirations at various points during the book. Also, I would like to thank Delhi, my birthplace, for being so vivid and inspiring.

And last but definitely not the least, my teachers, particularly my English teachers who inculcated in me the habit of reading & consequently writing.

Nishtha Chatterjee, is an MBA from the University of Wales and has been hobnobbing with Japanese people and their culture for almost a decade now, working in a corporate environment as a bilingual resource. She likes what she does for a living, but writing is another passion which suddenly came to the foreground thanks to her mundane job and some good-willed pestering from her family, who have an intuitive belief in her writing talent.

Nishtha loves to experiment with food both on her tongue & in the kitchen. She also loves being around dogs, her little bundles of joy who jump out from every nook and corner as soon as she walks the street. 'Pyaar se peyt nahi bharta' is her first written endeavour apart from the innumerable tutorials & dissertations she has written during her student days.

Nishtha can be reached at nishthachatterjee@gmail.com

She can also be followed on https://www.facebook.com/nishtha.chatterjee